PRAISE FOR THE
MYSTERIES

"Pandian launches a supernatural cozy series that hits high marks for a modern twist on an ancient practice. Amusing supporting characters and historical details solidify this engaging mystery." —*Library Journal*

"Pandian sets this series apart from other paranormal mysteries with Zoe's cute nonhuman sidekick and some mouthwatering vegan recipes." —*Publishers Weekly*

"This new series is off to an excellent start with an intriguing, eccentric amateur detective... This reviewer is eagerly anticipating more from this series, and a return of a cast more fun than an episode of Portlandia."
—*RT Book Reviews*

"Zoe and Dorian are my new favorite amateur-sleuth duo!"
—Victoria Laurie, *New York Times* bestselling author

"*The Accidental Alchemist* is a recipe for a great read. Gigi Pandian's pen never disappoints."
—Juliet Blackwell, *New York Times* bestselling author of the Witchcraft Mystery Series

"Mysterious, captivating, and infused with the rich history of the Northwest...fantastic." —*Portland Book Review*

"Readers won't want to put this book down."
— *Vegetarian Journal*

The Lost Gargoyle of Paris

An Accidental Alchemist Mystery Novella

By Gigi Pandian

Gargoyle Girl Productions

Cover design by Gargoyle Girl Productions
Cover gargoyle illustration by Hugh D'Andrade/Jennifer Vaughn Artist Agent

BOOKS BY GIGI PANDIAN

The Accidental Alchemist Mystery Series
The Accidental Alchemist
The Masquerading Magician
The Elusive Elixir
The Alchemist's Illusion

Jaya Jones Treasure Hunt Mystery Series
Artifact
Pirate Vishnu
Quicksand
Michelangelo's Ghost
The Ninja's Illusion
The Glass Thief

Locked-room mystery short story collection
The Cambodian Curse & Other Stories

ONE

"As one watched, the utter brilliance of the flame set them in motion. There were serpents that appeared to be laughing, gargoyles one seemed to hear yapping, salamanders blowing into the flames, dragons sneezing in the smoke."
—Victor Hugo, *Notre-Dame de Paris*

The fire began in a high crevice of the cathedral known as "the forest." On a cool spring evening, the scorching heat of the flames caught hold of the wood and crept through the innards of the Gothic structure. Silently. Invisibly. Until it was too late.

He watched in rapt attention, like everyone else. And immediately hated himself for it. He didn't think of himself as being anything like them.

Anyone standing beyond the western courtyard of Notre Dame Cathedral would have been forgiven for believing the medieval church was constructed entirely of stone, and therefore incapable of burning. In fact, the latticework roof and frame had been built out of the wood of thousands of oak trees. He learned, afterward, that the most common estimates ranged from 5,000 to 13,000 ancient oak trees. He usually valued precision, above all else, yet the wide range of guesses was forgivable, he decided, considering the wooden frame was one of the oldest surviving parts of the original building. The cathedral had been constructed nearly 800 years ago.

The names of the original architects and their records were long ago lost to history.

But not the names of the men involved in the nineteenth-century restoration. Those men were remembered. Architect, artist, and restorer Eugène Viollet-le-Duc breathed new life into the crumbling church, and kept meticulous records of all those involved, from *charpentièrs* to *tailleurs de pierre,* and everything in between those carpenters building scaffolding and the stonemasons carving gargoyles.

And he couldn't forget the man initially responsible for saving the cathedral. Novelist Victor Hugo, whose prose captured the collective imagination of the citizens of France and propelled the restoration forward. Hugo imagined a romantic medieval cathedral that had, in truth, never existed. Quasimodo could never have lurked among such a wide array of gargoyles and chimeras, because they hadn't been there. Not until Hugo imagined them in his fiction.

The stones had weathered centuries of natural erosion from rainwater and pollution, architectural disagreements about what form the cathedral's various restorations would take, and purposeful destruction from both idealistic revolutionaries and Nazi occupiers. If only the gargoyles could have cried out as their claws warmed with heat and their throats choked on smoke, perhaps they could have sounded the alarm before it was too late. By the time the thick gray smoke openly billowed around the famous limestone gargoyles added to the cathedral in the 1800s, the heroic firefighters were powerless to save the roof and spire.

It was those stones that gave him the idea. As he watched the billowing plumes of smoke, he couldn't help smiling.

He didn't feel entirely *good* about feeling giddy with happiness at the destruction. He wasn't a monster, after all. But he was about to become a very rich man.

TWO

I knew it had been a terrible mistake to relinquish my bag when I checked into my flight. Especially with my best friend curled up inside it.

My heel tapped nervously on the shiny white floor as my eyes darted around the baggage claim carousel at Charles de Gaulle airport in Paris. I held my breath each time a new set of bags thumped from the luggage chute onto the conveyor belt.

Nothing.

Around me, tourists chattered about visiting the Eiffel Tower, the Louvre, or the Musée D'Orsay. Two young travelers standing near me fantasized about the nightclubs, and I lamented the fact that neither they nor anyone else would ever again be able to visit Paris's best nightclub. *Cabaret de l'Enfer* in Monmartre had been opened in 1892 but closed in 1950. You can now find a department store on the spot it once stood. Yes, I'm a lot older than I look. A few hundred years older, in fact.

I'm as human as everyone else, so I would have loved to explore Paris like a tourist, but fun wasn't in the cards for this trip. But still… this was *Paris*. It was impossible not to be pulled into the unique energy of the city. Even here at the airport with the squeaky gray and white floors at baggage claim. Localities hold their own unique energy. It's why alchemists like me have always been drawn to cities like Paris and Prague. And why I was drawn to Portland last year when I rolled into town.

But I wasn't here to reminisce about my path becoming an accidental alchemist. Dorian and I knew a secret about Notre Dame. If we were right about what the recent fire had revealed, we might have a very messy mystery to solve.

Still, no sign of my suitcase. No sign of Dorian.

Plenty of passengers hadn't yet received their bags. There was no reason to think anything had happened. Except that it was Dorian. Something *always* happened.

He'd insisted on coming with me to Paris. Which was fair enough. He was even more distraught than I was about the fire that had swept through Notre Dame Cathedral, its fiery tentacles creeping stealthily across hidden wooden beams until the roof was destroyed and the towering spire collapsed.

Though I'd lived in Paris many years ago, Dorian was the one whose life was tied to the cathedral. He was born here in Paris, inside the workshop where the tradesmen skilled in carving stone were restoring the cathedral under Eugène Viollet-le-Duc's supervision.

Dorian's "birth" wasn't like most of ours. He's a gargoyle. Which is why I let him convince me it was OK for him to curl his wings around himself, step into my suitcase, and turn to stone for the duration of the trip from Portland to Paris.

Yes, as much as I've always wanted a normal life—and I'd made great inroads this past year—there was still a lot that defied normality in my life these days. I knew the checked bag was the quickest and safest way to get Dorian to Paris. It's not like I could buy a plane ticket for a living gargoyle.

And yes, technically Dorian is a *chimera*. He'd originally been carved in stone to be one of the creatures who looked down from the balustrade of Notre Dame, not a stone head with a lead pipe waterspout in his mouth to drain water from the roof. But nobody uses the word chimera. Not even Dorian. Although the word gargoyle narrowly describes architectural details with waterspouts as mouths, the term has become a catch-all for the stone creatures that adorn old buildings.

As for my particular gargoyle? He was every bit as impish and mischievous as you'd imagine if you've ever caught a glimpse of a stone creature above and wondered, just for a moment, whether he was watching you.

Which is why I'd wanted to keep Dorian close at hand in my carry-on bag. But in addition to the fact that I wasn't entirely sure even a gargoyle could contort himself to fit into the minuscule confines of a carry-on, this was an international flight. Meaning weight restrictions. Dorian simply weighed too much. Perhaps it was because he was originally made of stone, but I had my suspicions that it had more to do with the fact that he was a gourmet chef who loved French haute cuisine.

"It's the only way," he'd said as we packed.

I gave in. You'd think I'd be less of a pushover after 340 years. Normally I don't have a problem staying resolute. My weakness is my best friend.

Still, I almost changed my mind about the trip when I saw that Dorian had packed two novels and three homemade baguette sandwiches. Mushroom and olive tapenade, caramelized onion hummus, and coconut oil butter with fig preserves. He was planning on getting up and having a picnic in the cargo hold. That's why I was so worried now. Had he left the suitcase and been seen? Was he unable to get back inside? No, even if that were the case, my suitcase would still show up, sans gargoyle.

I drank the last few sips of the lemon water in my water bottle and glanced from the baggage carousel to the billboards advertising luxury products and Paris tourism. One was advertising for the newly opened Victor Hugo museum exhibit—the reason I was in Paris.

A detailed sketch of a Notre Dame gargoyle by novelist Victor Hugo himself had been discovered in the wreckage left behind after the fire. The press had dubbed the drawing "The Lost Gargoyle of Paris."

The illustration was hidden behind a stone laid during the mid-nineteenth-century restoration that had been dislodged during the fire. The paper was tucked inside a narrow leather journal belonging to one of the men who'd worked on the nineteenth-century restoration. On the cover of the journal was what looked very much like an alchemical symbol—an *ouroboros,* a serpent eating its own tail in the form of a circle, representing eternity. The gargoyle illustration tucked inside the journal was worn with age and badly damaged, but enough of it remained to identify it as being drawn by Victor Hugo.

On the surface, the discovery was incredibly exciting. A symbol of resilience at a time when it was much needed. I knew firsthand how frequently pieces of history get forgotten—or worse, purposefully covered up. But I also couldn't ignore the danger. There were backward alchemists who would go to extreme measures to get their hands on a discovery that included not only alchemy, but the energy of a creative genius. If any of the backward alchemists were still alive, it was a combination they wouldn't be able to pass up.

The black rubber segments of the conveyor belt squeaked to a grinding halt, yanking me back to the present. The last bags and the remaining passengers around me were all gone.

I forgot about the billboard. I had bigger problems. No Dorian.

"*Mademoiselle*?" The voice came from a young airport employee striding towards me at a brisk clip. "*Pardon.* Are you, by chance, Zoe Faust?" he asked in formal French.

"Yes," I answered in English. Not because my French was rusty (although it was) but because I didn't want to arouse suspicions that I was anyone other than who I was supposed to be. Twenty-eight-year-old American Zoe Faust, who'd recently bought a fixer-upper craftsman house in Portland, Oregon, after living out of my Airstream trailer for several years. Employment status: Like many millennials, I ran my own online business. My online store Elixir sold funky antique items, which I didn't mention weren't antique at all when I'd purchased them in person a century or so before. I also didn't correct people who assumed I dyed my hair white to be trendy. It began turning white naturally nearly 300 years ago when I was in my 30s.

"Your identification?" The young man looked down his nose at me as he raised his open palm, waiting impatiently.

I handed him my passport. The passport itself wasn't a forgery. Only the birth certificate I'd used to obtain it.

"*Merci*. We have something that belongs to you."

"You found my bag?"

"It is the strangest thing. It became separated from the other luggage during the flight. The baggage area was in disarray. This one looked as though it might have been opened, so we inspected it."

My low-level anxiety kicked up a notch. The last vestige of fatigue was instantly replaced with fiery fear. "You—"

"I believe I understand why you brought this statue."

"You do?" I croaked.

"It looks very much like the famous gargoyle who watches over us from Notre Dame, *n'est-ce pas*?" His formal manner shifted. He smiled as he spoke the word *gargoyle*.

I returned the smile. "Indeed he does. So… my bag?"

"*Un moment*," he said, and returned less than a minute later rolling the suitcase at his side. "You are quite talented."

"The gargoyle?"

"Such detail in the stone."

I shook my head. "I can't claim credit for carving him."

"Is he for display at the Victor Hugo exhibition? It's quite exciting, *n'est-ce pas*?"

"Not for display," I said, choosing my words carefully, "but yes, the terrible fire at the cathedral is why I wanted to bring him—*er,* it—to Paris."

"To think that Notre Dame's stones held such secrets."

He didn't know the half of it.

"Perhaps," he continued, "you should find a more secure way of shipping such an exquisite creature."

"He was damaged?" Oh no… What would happen to Dorian if he was injured while in stone form? I knelt in front of the hard case, inspecting it for dents, but saw none.

"I did not mean to distress you, *mademoiselle. Ne vous inquiètez pas.* We found nothing amiss, and your statue had not broken. Was it by chance a turbulent flight?"

"Yes," I said. "It was definitely a turbulent flight."

The trip was about to get even more turbulent. I'd traveled across the globe because I had a creeping suspicion that backward alchemists would try to steal Victor Hugo's Lost Gargoyle of Paris.

THREE

Marcel Boucher was my best lead. He wasn't an alchemist. At least, I was fairly certain that was the case. The sixty-year-old historian's photograph that accompanied his online CV looked like that of a much younger man, but I attributed the discrepancy to the fact that people rarely update their headshots.

I didn't know Professor Boucher personally. Shortly after the Lost Gargoyle of Paris discovery was revealed, his words were quoted extensively by several news sources, when media outlets were desperate for anyone they could call an "expert" to speculate about the fire. What I found so interesting about Marcel Boucher's comments was that he was the only expert to be publicly *skeptical* of the discovery.

Yet after several prominent features were published, his dissenting voice was silenced. All references to Marcel Boucher were stripped from the online versions of the articles. The only reason I remembered his name was because Dorian insisted on subscribing to the print edition of *Le Monde*.

What was being covered up?

Before leaving the airport and meeting the professor, I needed to make sure Dorian was safe. My suitcase was heavy enough that it felt like he was inside, but I hadn't detected any movement coming from the bag since the airport worker had handed it off to me.

I dragged the hefty suitcase across the floor of the sprawling baggage claim. Even with wheels, the suitcase didn't roll fast enough for comfort. As I looked in vain for a spot with a modicum of privacy, the gray and white striped floor seemed to be leading me through a labyrinth that I was unable to escape.

With no privacy to be found, I took another approach. I sat down in a chair near a large tour group, half of whom were listening to their exasperated guide and half of whom were scrolling on their cell phones. I maneuvered my suitcase directly in front of me, took out my phone, and popped my earbud headphones into my ears.

"Dorian!" I said, holding my phone in front of my face. "How are you?"

"You are not going to help me out of this prison?" a deep, muffled, French-accented voice asked from within the suitcase.

"It's so good to talk with you on the phone." I held the phone closer to my mouth, which was completely unnecessary since nobody was paying attention to us. "I'm glad to find a moment here at this crowded airport."

"Ah, so. *Je comprends*. I am an 'exquisite creature,' after all."

I rolled my eyes, even though nobody was watching me. "I wanted to make sure you didn't need anything before I get a cab to the apartment."

I heard a distinct sniff. Oh no… He was injured and trying not to worry me. Another sniff came from within the suitcase. I was about to peek inside, throwing caution to the wind, when he spoke.

"I smell croissants. *Freshly baked* croissants. If you could procure—"

"The apartment has a kitchen, remember?" He was fine. That's all I needed to know. "I'll buy groceries. We'll be eating soon enough."

"Alchemists," he mumbled, "with their misguided belief that patience is a virtue..."

Dorian Robert-Houdin—before he was christened Dorian—was once a stone chimera carved by hand out of limestone from the Seine basin. He was meant to become one of the new stone creatures envisioned by Eugène Viollet-le-Duc during the restoration of Notre Dame in the mid-1800s. Unfortunately, the architect realized the prototype was too small. The carving's three-and-a-half foot stature was deemed too tiny to see from the courtyard below, so the size of the gargoyles was increased.

Rather than discard the stone carving with a mischievous glint in its eyes, Viollet-le-Duc gave the sculpture to his friend Jean Eugène Robert-Houdin. The famous stage magician gratefully accepted the gift from his architect friend, imagining the little creature with such personality, even in stone, would be a wonderful stage prop. He never suspected that a book of alchemy he read from to create a dramatic scene on stage contained real magic. Nor that the alchemical power was linked to the alchemists who practiced a corrupt and unstable form of alchemy in secrecy—below Notre Dame Cathedral in Paris.

Beyond being a sacred place of worship and a secular symbol of France, Notre Dame was much more than most people realized. Among countless other secrets I had no doubt were hidden within its stone walls and wooden beams, the 800-year-old cathedral's secret connection to alchemy was hidden in plain sight. If a person looked closely at the Christian imagery, they would be rewarded by finding multiple alchemical symbols. A salamander escaping flames unscathed could be found on the cathedral's façade, symbolizing the Secret Fire. A ladder of seven steps symbolized the steps alchemists followed. And one of the carved saints was defeating a dragon that was actually an ouroboros, the serpent curled in a circle swallowing his own tail, representing alchemy's cyclical processes.

So I wasn't surprised there was the alchemical symbol of an ouroboros on the cover of the stonemason's notebook. It didn't mean he'd been an alchemist, or that Victor Hugo was. But symbols have power. And as a creative genius in multiple art forms—a novelist, poet, and artist—Hugo possessed a vibrant energy the backward alchemists would love to feed on, especially since his creation had been nestled alongside alchemical energy for so many years.

Energy and transformation are at the heart of all forms of alchemy. A person's focused intent can create transformations that change an impure metal into pure gold, a wilting plant into a healing elixir, and a mortal body into one that ceases aging. I used my own energy and intent when I practiced alchemy, but not everyone was willing to put in the effort required, and instead sought shortcuts.

Backward alchemists took fundamental concepts of alchemy and distorted them. They believed they could use destructive shortcuts to achieve transformations—by stealing the energy of others. They'd nearly killed a dear friend of mine last year. I was now confident that they'd lost all their power, but what if I was wrong?

So here I was in Paris with a rogue gargoyle, having left behind my loved ones and the precariously comfortable life I'd forged for myself in Portland. I had to make sure the backward alchemists hadn't returned.

FOUR

"Nothing makes a man so adventurous as an empty pocket."
— Victor Hugo, Notre-Dame de Paris

It was his relationship with Paloma that made it possible. Not that they were romantically involved—he shuddered at the thought.

Paloma had grown up in Paris, which is why he'd first spent time with her at a cocktail party the previous year. He'd needed some specific information, and she'd given it to him without realizing she'd done so.

She was angular, he mused, in every way. Her nose, cheeks, and extra long toes that he learned made her prefer sandals even in winter. Her apartment matched her body, with uncomfortable modernist white plastic chairs and gray slate tabletops. Her artistic vision was the most angular of all, with harsh strokes of her pen meant to fall within the modernist school of Picasso but instead mimicking a child's etch-a-sketch.

He'd seen her earlier work, before she'd developed her own distinctive style. It was good. She was a more than competent artist. It wasn't only an opinion. He'd studied art. It was a pity Paloma hadn't chosen to embrace her natural talents.

Paloma had always believed she'd been overlooked as an artist. She talked about it incessantly to anyone who would listen. And he was a very good listener. It never ceased to amaze him how much people would reveal to you if you simply let them talk. A few questions here and there, most of the time simply repeating the last few words someone said, but with the intonation of a question, was all it took.

"Your great great grandfather was one of the stonemasons who worked on Notre Dame's restoration?"

She'd turned beet red when he spoke those words. That was interesting. He'd only repeated what she'd just told him. He'd disarmed her and she'd said more than she meant to.

"Not *exactly* a stonemason," she'd admitted, her cheeks still a dark shade of pink. "He was one of the day laborers hired to help build scaffolding. His true artistic abilities were never realized during his lifetime." Her lips pursed as she spat out the words. "Just like mine have been overlooked."

"What if I could change that?" he'd asked her. He knew what her answer would be.

It would take time, of course. But like any good plan, it took time to do it right.

FIVE

It was a stressful cab ride to the center of the city. As the late morning traffic inched forward, I tried not to think about the fact that a gargoyle was being jostled in the trunk of the car. I couldn't let him out of the suitcase until we reached the apartment we'd rented, but I knew I'd never hear the end of it.

My body ached with the fatigue of a long-legged woman who's been sitting on two sleepless, long flights to Paris stuck in the economy cabin. I know, I know, if I listened to Dorian I'd simply make some gold. I was an alchemist, after all. But here's the thing. I've always been terrible at making gold. I'm much better with plants than minerals. Unfortunately, even though I can whip up one of the best green smoothies on the West Coast and coax any edible herb or vegetable in a kitchen garden back to life, those skills don't buy a first-class plane ticket.

The cab driver gave a dignified grunt as he lifted the suitcase out of the car in front of the apartment we'd rented with a view of Notre Dame. The whole building was apartment rentals, and all of them had been booked except for the tiny studio on the top floor. Every other affordable room close to the cathedral was occupied, but it was important for us to be as close as possible to the cathedral for our investigation.

I heaved the suitcase up the three stone steps into the building, and entered the code to the lockbox to get our keys. Inside, I pulled open the squeaking retracting metal grate of the 1940s elevator. Those things always make me feel as if I'm in a cage. But in this case, it was better than lugging the Dorian suitcase up six flights of stairs. I contorted myself around the hulking suitcase and pressed the button for the highest floor it went to, which the listing had warned was one floor below the top floor. The shoebox-sized lift lurched upward, its gears badly in need of grease.

When the elevator banged to a stop a minute later, a handsome, smartly dressed man stood in front of us. He blinked at me in surprise and stumbled backward, nearly tripping over his shoes, which looked more expensive than my entire wardrobe. I ran a hand through my white hair, the only part of me that had aged since I'd discovered the Elixir of Life. I hadn't taken a second glance at myself in the airplane toilet's tiny mirror, but I didn't think my disheveled state deserved his shocked retreat.

He chuckled at himself and shook his head, then stepped forward as I swung open the elevator cage door.

"*Bonjour,*" he said with an American accent. He recovered his manners and held open the metal door for me.

"Thank you," I replied, pulling the suitcase over the gap to the landing.

"A fellow American!"

My smile tightened. I should have stuck to French. Normally I'm a friendly person who laments how busy people are these days, but I didn't have time to be social. "An exhausted one, I'm afraid. Long flight, so I just want to get to my—"

"I thought I'd met everyone staying in the building already, and didn't think anyone else was on this floor—I'd definitely have remembered you." He tilted his head and gave me a smile that I'm sure had charmed many. It probably would have had more of an effect on me if I hadn't been so preoccupied by checking on Dorian and getting to work.

"Just arrived." I nodded at the suitcase at my side. "I really should get going—"

"Would you like help with your bag? Looks a bit unruly." He reached for the handle of the rolling bag with Dorian inside.

"Thanks, but we're going up." I slid the bag out of his reach as I tried for the third time to make my escape.

His smile faltered as he looked at the narrow winding steps leading to the top room, which was definitely more an attic than a penthouse, but he rallied. "No kidding. I didn't know they rented out the attic. Those stairs look tricky. You sure I can't help?"

He took my hesitation as an answer, and stepped forward and lifted the suitcase by its handle. "Hm? Did you say something?"

"No." I scowled at the bag. "I didn't say anything. But I did want to say thanks for the help." I was being too hard on the enthusiastic guy who meant well. He didn't abandon the bag once he realized how heavy it was, but he was winded by the time he reached my door.

I pushed open the solid door of the cozy (in other words: minuscule) apartment, and we were welcomed with dim light and a musty scent. Moth balls and smoke, with a hint of roses. The light shone through the only window in the apartment. Small, but big enough for the beam of light to illuminate the dust motes we'd be sharing the apartment with. I had a feeling I'd be drinking a lot of peppermint tea.

"Could I trouble you," he said between breaths, "for a glass of water?" He grinned sheepishly.

"Of course." I found a light switch and located a set of glass cups in the cabinet, smiling to myself with the familiar comfort of how drinking vessels in France were so much smaller than in the U.S., and filled it with tap water from the small sink.

"Some of us are having drinks in the building's courtyard at sunset." He paused to finish the water in two gulps. "You're more than welcome, if you'd like to join us." He gave me a roguish smile that I'm sure he thought young women—which he assumed I was—found irresistible.

"I'll be busy later, but thanks for the invitation."

He handed the empty glass back to me with thanks, gave a single nod, and disappeared down the stairs. I smiled as I watched the back of his head. From the back, he looked a bit like Max, with his black hair and slim-fitting dress shirt. I missed my boyfriend, but it was still too early in the morning in Portland to call him.

"Are you quite done with your new admirer?" Dorian began after the apartment door clicked shut, his voice still muffled by the suitcase.

"Let me get the curtains closed."

I strode to the solitary window to close the curtains and prevent prying eyes. In spite of the grumbling gargoyle inside the cramped suitcase, I couldn't resist taking a brief glance out the window. My breath caught as my gaze fell on the cathedral. The stone portions had survived the fire, so from a distance it was possible to imagine it stood as it had for centuries, weathering revolutions, ransacking, and the ravages of time. Nothing had gutted it so quickly as this year's fire.

"It's safe for you to come out," I said, feeling my heart in my throat as I closed the window. I hadn't sensed any negative energy of backward alchemy, or alchemy at all. Would I? I was jet-lagged, inside a dusty apartment, and though I could see the cathedral I wasn't yet on its grounds.

"*Ça fait un voyage trop long*," Dorian muttered. The suitcase zipper eased open. A gray face the texture of soft stone appeared. Liquidy black eyes glared up at me. He reached a clawed hand out of the bag and unzipped the suitcase the rest of the way. The top popped open as he unfurled his gray wings. A cross between the soft feathers of a bird and the hard edges of a stone gargoyle, the wings resembled those of an angel. He shook them out and stamped his clawed feet, ruining the effect.

In 1844, French architect-restorers Eugène Viollet-Le-Duc and his partner Jean Baptiste Lassus won the winning bid to restore the decaying cathedral. It was during the restoration efforts in the mid-1840s through the 1860s that the gallery of gargoyles was born. Controversial at the time, now nobody could imagine the cathedral without the stone chimeras looking out over the city from the balustrade.

As the tendrils of smoke and fire surrounded them, the chimeras that perched on the balustrade of the gallery of gargoyles, where thousands of tourists visited them each day, had no choice but to remain stoically in place.

That included the most famous gargoyle of all. Most people in the Western world would recognize his image. The melancholy face looking out over the city, his back slightly hunched with stone wings folded behind him, his hands resting on his chin as if in contemplation. He'd been called many names over the centuries—*le Stryge* (the vampire), the Devil of Paris, the Demon of Notre Dame.

I like to think of him by the name my friend Dorian Robert-Houdin favors: *le Penseur*. The Thinker. The stone creature's contemplative, melancholy pose certainly suggests the name. Plus, it's a more honorable moniker than vampire, devil, or demon. For the gargoyles of Notre Dame aren't evil. They're simply stones that represent many things to many people.

Most of them, at least, are only figurative representations carved into unmoving stone. Except for the ones that had been accidentally brought to life through alchemy.

"I do not recommend this form of travel," Dorian muttered. "Perhaps we could buy a steamer trunk for our return trip. One with a release mechanism to open the lid from the inside, like a magician would use—"

"I'm going to ignore the fact that you ransacked the cargo area of the flight."

"Ransack? *Non.* I did not ransack. I simply moved a few bags so I could comfortably read the novel that has brought us to Paris." He clutched a weathered paperback copy of Victor Hugo's *Notre-Dame de Paris,* the French title of *The Hunchback of Notre Dame,* in his hand. "If you were a better alchemist, able to turn lead into gold, we could afford to donate to the cause to rebuild the cathedral."

I scowled down at Dorian. "You're a real alchemist now too. You know how difficult it is to make gold." I crossed my arms and fiddled with the sleeves of my sweater. I might have been a little bit touchy about my inability to make gold.

"I have only *recently* learned true alchemy, Zoe Faust. How can you expect me—"

"We're not having this argument right now. I need to meet with that scholar about the Lost Gargoyle of Paris illustration, and then you and I can visit the cathedral to see if the backward alchemists are back."

Dorian pointed a claw toward the sliver of sunlight at the edge of the curtains. "Before dark?"

I grinned. "I have a plan."

SIX

"This is a most terrible plan," the gargoyle whined. "*Most* terrible."

Dorian didn't like my plan because it didn't *first* involve my going to the market for food.

Our flight had landed at 10 o'clock in the morning, so we had nearly a full day ahead of us. I established my priorities.

First, I'd meet with the historian who'd been silenced.

Second, I'd take Dorian with me to visit the cathedral, a feat that was possible because I'd devised the perfect disguise. Only then would we know the urgency of the situation. After that we could determine a plan for food.

And finally, at the end of the day, I had a ticket to visit the Victor Hugo exhibit, where I'd case the place. Which wasn't as nefarious as it sounded. I wanted to carefully inspect the security to determine if the backward alchemists were an additional risk. I wasn't arrogant enough to think I was better at security than trained professionals. But I was a fellow alchemist. I could anticipate their thought process better than someone looking for modern thieves.

Alchemists think differently. They don't accept the world for what it is. They *transform* things. Turning lead into gold is the most commonly known example of what we can do, but that's such a tiny sliver of what's possible.

The reason this was the last item on my agenda was because since the Victor Hugo exhibit had only just opened, and being in high demand, all the tickets were time-stamped. I'd wanted to visit as soon as we landed in Paris, but I couldn't be sure if our flight would be late, so I'd booked the last slot of the day.

"Sustenance," Dorian continued, "is the key to our life force. One cannot be expected to fight evil alchemists without... *Mon dieu!* Did you see—?" Dorian broke off and clasped his clawed hands together with glee.

He'd spotted the kitchen.

"*Bon,*" Dorian continued. "I did not know if she was to be believed about the state of the kitchen. Small, yet serviceable." He scampered to the kitchen and surveyed the space.

Dorian had been the one to pick out the apartment. Or rather, he'd sweet-talked his way into this rental. Dorian knew the best locations to get a close-up view of the cathedral, which would be important if we were right about the backward alchemists. This building was the only rental property that fit the criteria. He wasn't going to let the fact that there were no available apartment rentals stop him. Dorian began an email correspondence with the property manager (a widow). He made up a saccharine story about his ailing health, his joy at his American granddaughter visiting, and how the two of them had climbed the 387 steps to visit the gargoyles of the cathedral. It would mean so much to them if his granddaughter—supposedly me—had a close view of the cathedral.

I wasn't surprised that he'd won her over and she'd opened up a room not normally available. Though Dorian's claws prevent him from using a cell phone screen, he's great with a keyboard. And in a kitchen.

He yanked on the door of the oven and grimaced. Pinching the bridge of his snout, he said, "I will require baking soda and vinegar when you visit the market."

#

I revised my opinion of Professor Marcel Boucher as soon as the massive wooden door to his office creaked open.

Large eyes blinked at me from above a full gray beard. I stifled a gasp. With his oversize dark eyes and a hooked nose overshadowed by a beard, he could have been the model for the most famous—and incorrect—portrait of my mentor, Nicolas Flamel, which had been painted after his supposed death. Nicolas, incidentally, looked nothing like that.

His eyes came to rest slightly above my eyes, on the roots of my white hair. The intensity and inquisitiveness of his gaze told me this was not a man to trifle with. *This* was a man who looked like an alchemist.

But looks can be deceiving.

"*Mademoiselle*?" he inquired.

"Professor Boucher? I'm Zoe Faust." I extended my hand.

"Ah!" He shook my hand and switched to English. "You wrote of your desire to meet today, but did not mention what time you'd stop by—"

He broke off abruptly. I could sense the "*and you don't look like what I expected*" hovering on his lips, though he was too polite to say it.

"Please, please come in," he added instead. He removed a stack of books from a high-backed chair in front of his desk and frowned as he looked around helplessly for an empty spot to place them.

It gave me time to remind myself that he'd aged at least a decade since his online headshot. Not an alchemist. At least not a *successful* one. So that wasn't why he was trying to dissuade the public about the authenticity of the discovery at Notre Dame.

"Please." He offered me the newly freed chair, having deposited the books on top of an already precariously high pile of books and papers. The smooth rosewood of the chair was hundreds of years old, and gold silk threads formed patterns reminiscent of tapestries on the azure cushion resting against the back. The space on his walls not crammed with bookshelves was filled with reproductions of paintings from Baroque to Neoclassical, as one would expect from an art historian. I again reminded myself that not everyone who appreciated history was an alchemist.

"Your email did not provide many details." He hitched up his trousers and sat down behind his oak desk—another piece of furniture assembled long before the professor had been born. "But when someone writes of history with such urgency?" He grinned, and his thin lips parted under his beard. "How could I resist such a request?"

"I thought it would be easier to speak in person. I'm curious about why you're a skeptic about the journal and illustration found in the rubble of the cathedral."

His large eyes widened. "You read those articles before they were deleted? I'm terribly sorry to disappoint you. I am no longer a skeptic."

"You're not?"

"The only thing I am skeptical of is our inefficient government."

"You don't believe the discovery is a fraud?"

"A fraud?" He tilted his head. A curious expression, not a defensive one. "Why would you say that?"

It was true that his remarks hadn't come right out and used the word fraud. But his words had definitely hinted at it. Something was off about the discovery. But what? The inside pages of the journal hadn't been publicized. Could there be alchemy inside, making normal people believe it to be a joke, or perhaps authentic but bad for publicity at a sacred church? I had to find out if the professor's skepticism was justified and meant that the backward alchemists were truly a danger.

"You were skeptical," I reminded him, perhaps too harshly, "that after all these years a hidden journal and valuable work of art would simply appear at a time when the cathedral was in desperate need of money."

"You misunderstood." Through his whiskers, a condescending smile formed on his lips. It was an expression I was far too familiar with, though I saw it less frequently in this century than in previous ones.

"I misunderstood the multiple articles in which you ranted about the problematic discovery." I tried to keep my voice neutral but wasn't at all sure that I succeeded.

"I wished to make the point that processes were not followed as they should have been following the fire. Not with the lead contamination. Not with the call for rebuilding more quickly than is humanly possible to do properly! And *not* with the authentication of the valuable work of art that will fetch a large sum of money." He spoke slowly at first, but his voice grew more animated as he progressed. "Official procedures exist for a reason. Not to be dismissed during a crisis. I was vilified for being the voice of reason."

"Oh."

"You look disappointed."

"Your skepticism backed up my initial reaction when I heard of the discovery. Something seemed off."

"What did you say your interest was?" The curiosity in his gaze was gone, as was his indignation. Now I was met with a cold gaze of mistrust.

"I run an antiques business, so I have a feeling when something isn't right about a historical item."

"A *feeling*," he repeated.

Well I wasn't going to tell him I'd been alive when Victor Hugo was writing and painting or that I knew some of the alchemists who'd practiced their trade underneath where the journal had been discovered.

He sighed. "I was gravely disappointed the journal and illustration were not immediately chemically authenticated. They appeared to be authentic, but I wanted them tested."

"Isn't it the case that most historical works of art are never chemically tested?"

He shifted uncomfortably. "In a case like this, it is for the best. Others agreed. My university asked for me to be silent until authentications were completed, and called in favors to have my statements removed. They did not wish to invite lawsuits. Since then, several experts authenticated the damaged illustration by sight. For the chemical test, they took a page from the journal."

"So it's real." And would be incredibly valuable to alchemists who sought the power of Notre Dame. I'd been hoping I was wrong about the danger. I'd been hoping for a different type of fraud. A publicity stunt, instead of true discoveries related to alchemy, would have made the discoveries irrelevant to alchemists.

The professor sighed. "I appreciate critical analysis from my students, so I suppose I'm being hard on you because of my own censure for speaking publicly of my outrage. What's the matter?"

"It worries me that something so valuable is at a small museum."

"You have not yet visited?"

I shook my head. "I have a ticket for later this afternoon."

"The security is quite adequate, I can assure you. Much more than adequate."

"Are visitors able to handle the journal? There haven't been many photographs of the inside of the journal online. I'm eager to see it."

He tilted his head again. This time accompanied by scratching his chin through his beard. "It is a museum display. Not an academic institution where scholars can handle the documents. Both the illustration and journal are behind glass."

"I suppose that's for the best." Sure, I'd have loved to get a closer look at the journal and its contents, but my primary concern was for its safety.

"But you just asked—"

"It's valuable, as you said. I'd hate to see anyone steal it."

The professor pursed his lips. "As I mentioned, it's quite secure. Thick glass cases are in place to prevent eager onlookers from damaging the fragile illustration. The glass will also prevent theft."

"Is it alarmed as well?"

"Alarmed?"

"There are definitely people who might want to steal the illustration."

"People? If you know something about a threat, we should alert—"

"I should go."

"But *mademoiselle*—"

"Thank you for your time." I should have taken Dorian's concerns about nourishing myself more seriously. I was tired and not as subtle as I should have been. I hurried down the hallway, not stopping when I heard him call my name.

SEVEN

"A one-eyed man is much more incomplete than a blind man, for he knows what it is that's lacking."
– Victor Hugo, Notre-Dame de Paris

He hated getting his hands dirty. Usually he could avoid it. But these were definitely dirty pictures. It was a good thing she didn't want her husband to see them.

He wasn't asking much of Brie. He was the one taking the bigger risk. Yet she had the audacity to try to negotiate and offer him money instead!

But now that was settled.

All this fuss over a single sheet of paper.

It always amazed him what people thought was valuable.

He'd eaten fugu in a small coastal town in Japan. He'd forgotten the name of the town and the restaurant, but remembered every sensation from the meal itself, from the superior stares of his stablemates who didn't believe he'd join them, to the rich, rubbery texture of the fish. But he knew the flavor wasn't the point. Russian roulette to prove your strength by risking your life to the poisonous puffer fish.

He'd seen a private collection of stolen Vermeer artwork, which were far too muddy and dark for his taste, not nearly as engaging as Van Meegren's knock-offs. But again, he understood the value to the man who kept his prized paintings hidden away.

And he'd danced with an heiress who was far more interesting before he'd realized her diamonds and gold were paste and pyrite.

But this was different. In this case, the Victor Hugo illustration *was* valuable to him.

Victor Hugo was special. He had revived French pride – a false pride, but more power to him. He, too, had a brief fling with law school before abandoning it for art.

Victor was celebrated for being a great French novelist and poet, but he made more drawings than any other type of artistic creation, accumulating a body of several thousand illustrations. It wasn't surprising to anyone that a gargoyle would be among the drawings.

Many an art historian had mused that if Hugo had devoted himself to the visual arts instead of literary arts, he could have been as celebrated a painter as Van Gogh.

But Victor hadn't only chosen to focus his time on literary pursuits. For many years, he actively hid his drawings. He didn't want them overshadowing his literature. Only when he cast his novels aside to focus on political activism did he let himself use drawing as his primary creative outlet.

In spite of his high profile literary success—or perhaps because of it—he found himself in exile from 1848 - 1851. That was when his artwork flourished the most.

Victor kept his creations small, never bigger than the size paper one would use to write a letter, and often as small as a calling card. His preferred medium was a black pen-and-ink wash, occasionally using brown ink, rarely adding additional color, but improvising and using coffee grounds if it was all that was on hand.

Now, a century and a half after Victor Hugo's death, this style and the secrecy of his artwork was about to make a modern man's wildest dreams come true. Everything was in place for the theft. All he had to do was wait for the exhibit in the museum down the street from Notre Dame Cathedral to open.

EIGHT

Though the fire had long since been extinguished, the smell of smoke still hung in the air. I stayed alert, looking for anyone I recognized—but desperately hoping I didn't see anyone. I didn't want to be recognized by an alchemist who might have been involved, so I'd taken the precaution of tucking my distinctive hair under a knit cap. I couldn't bear to part with my favorite silver raincoat, though. It wasn't only the fact that it was the perfect garment for chilly weather. I loved it, so I felt stronger in it. Which was a feeling I badly needed after my blunder with Marcel Boucher. I hoped he couldn't trace where I was staying, or surely he'd send the police to question me.

I pushed the rented wheelchair across the street and into the western courtyard, dodging two scooters as I went. Thankfully, Dorian had agreed to the disguise. In an old dress, two shawls, and a scarf covering his head and neck, plus a fashionable wide-brimmed hat, he was my petite grandmother. I had packed the large swaths of fabric in the checked bag with Dorian, leading him to believe it was for cushioning. I thought it would be easier to convince him to don the disguise once we reached Paris. I was right.

What I wasn't right about was how close to the cathedral we'd be able to get. We'd only barely entered the courtyard, and I wouldn't be able to take us much further. Barricades and scaffolding blocked off most of the once-vast courtyard in front of the majestic stone towers that were now missing their spire behind them.

As evidenced by the flock of people surrounding us, the cathedral was in the hearts of many. And now that Professor Boucher had confirmed that the discovery of the journal and the Lost Gargoyle of Paris illustration were authentic, the cathedral would be in the hearts and minds of backward alchemists as well.

"My poor brothers," Dorian murmured, his head craned upward toward the stone gargoyles. "And you. Now that the art historian believes you to be a suspicious person, why are you wearing that shiny silver coat? It is like a beacon."

I didn't feel like explaining it served the purpose of a security blanket, so I tightened the silver belt and pushed the wheelchair toward the cathedral. As we drew closer to the barricades, my hands began to shake. I let go of the handles and rubbed them together, even though it wasn't cold I was feeling.

"Something is wrong," Dorian whispered from beneath the folds of fabric.

I knelt beside the wheelchair. "We knew the cathedral would be closed off."

"That is not what I speak of. You are ill. Is it the backward alchemists? Have they poisoned the area?" He attempted to turn his head to look around, but instead tightened the scarf wrapped around his neck up to his snout.

He was right that I was ill, but not about the cause. A heavy weight of exhaustion crept into my bones as we entered the western courtyard, growing stronger with each step. It wasn't the jet lag. It wasn't the emotional stress of seeing the devastation up close. Those were both slowly taking their toll, but they weren't what hit me like a swirling tornado I couldn't escape.

I felt the lead.

The area had been decontaminated, so I wasn't worried about lead poisoning, but because my body is hyper-attuned to nature and the elements, I can sense trace amounts of substances that most people can't, such as detecting a scent of poison that's supposedly undetectable. That skill had gotten me in trouble more times than I could count, and even worse is the fact that I get tired as soon as the sun goes down (I'm a terrible date). But it's also how I can coax plants back to life even when most people take them for dead, and how I can do a bit of good for people themselves through my knowledge of herbalism.

Much of the lead in the cathedral burned in the intense flames, the billowing smoke carrying the particles to the surrounding areas. Authorities had sprung into action (not as quickly as some would have liked) but elements always leave a trace.

I first saw Notre Dame de Paris in the year 1700, long before the famous gargoyles were in place—and several years before I discovered the Elixir of Life. I was twenty-four, though even now I don't consider myself to have been young at the time. My innocence had dissipated nearly a decade before, when those I loved and trusted betrayed me. They accused me of being a witch because I was so good with coaxing life from struggling plants, both in our kitchen garden and the crops on larger plots of land. I fled from Massachusetts to Europe, and used my aptitude with plants to sell healing tinctures to get by, until my creations caught the attention of Nicolas Flamel. I traveled from England to France to begin an apprenticeship with the famous alchemist.

Nicolas and his wife Perenelle maintained residences in both Paris and the countryside. My apprenticeship was to take place in the country, but I first visited Paris. The city was like nothing I'd seen before, and Notre Dame was the North Star shining in a bright night sky. It had been breathtaking then, its grace and history astounding regardless of whether you viewed it as a secular monument or a religious sanctuary. It was simultaneously a holy site and a symbol of French resilience.

"I'll be all right." I took a sip of the nettle tea in the thermos in my shoulder bag.

I was devastated by the scale of the destruction in front of me. I didn't sense any negative energy of backward alchemists—alchemy isn't magic, after all. But I did wonder if I was wrong that they'd attempt to steal the discovery. Even though it would be of use to them, they were such lazy, lazy people. That's why they'd latched onto a false alchemy that wasn't a fraction as much work. But it was also why they'd want a precious illustration that had been nestled untouched in an alchemy-infused journal for more than a century. I couldn't dismiss the threat. I took another sip of tea, put the cap back on the thermos, and stood up.

"You are better? *Bon.* Push me closer, Zoe."

"If you hadn't noticed, I can't."

"*I can't,* says the woman who found the Elixir of Life when she was 28 years old! Younger, I might add, than any man has achieved."

"Flattery won't move those barricades."

"Flattery, like the saints in this cathedral, has created many miracles. Did you hear any of them saying, *I cannot, it is trop difficile?"*

I couldn't see Dorian's eyes beneath the shawl he'd wrapped around his head and the wide-brimmed hat I'd insisted on. But I would have bet the entire contents of my alchemy laboratory, including my hard-to-come-by gold, that he was scowling at me.

I turned the wheelchair and guided Dorian closer. I wanted to hear what a guard was saying to a group of tourists. We reached the edge of the group as he was explaining the importance of the barricades. The tourists insisted they'd seen photos on social media of people who'd been able to get closer. The patient guard explained that the fences put in place after the fire had been placed different distances from the cathedral at different times since the fire, as the situation was assessed and workers began clearing out the debris.

"Closer," Dorian whined.

Honestly, sometimes I wasn't sure if he was a 160-year-old or a teenager.

Dorian began to squirm and make choking noises.

"Are you all right, madame?" the guard knelt and spoke in French, leaving the gaggle of frustrated tourists as he spoke to Dorian.

"My *grandmère* has lost her teeth," I answered for him, "so she has difficulty speaking. She's only distressed because it would mean so much to her to get closer. I don't suppose—"

"*Je suis désolé, mademoiselle*. It is too dangerous. As I was explaining, nobody is allowed further. May I suggest a view from across the river, perhaps in the courtyard in front of the bookshop." He gestured toward Shakespeare & Company.

"*Merci*."

"You are giving up?" Dorian whispered as I turned the wheelchair.

"We'll stick to our original plan."

"Ah, so. *La nuit*. We shall resume our search in the night."

"With my map of the catacombs."

NINE

"The Middle Ages believed him to be the cathedral's demon.
In fact he was its soul."
– Victor Hugo, Notre-Dame de Paris

The gargoyles loomed high above them. The stones cast eerie shadows in the darkness. Watching as a lookout with binoculars, he could almost imagine Quasimodo lurking among the stone creatures.

He couldn't have done this without Lucy. In addition to the part she still had to play, Little Lucy had been the one to go to the catacombs.

He knew that many people had died there. There was no way he was going himself. But he was an expert at convincing others that his interests were theirs. He didn't have to ask Lucy for a favor. She truly believed she was the best person for the job.

The labyrinthine tunnels were far more dangerous than the tourist photos would have you believe. Beyond the rooms of human skulls that were a macabre tourist attraction, or the vast caves that provide an exciting atmosphere for raves or art exhibits, hundreds of miles of tunnels stretch beneath the city. Nobody knew them all. Burrowing had been going on as far back as the Middle Ages, when the limestone was quarried. Quarries gave way to catacombs and crypts, and in the modern era, sewers and the metro.

It might be exciting to be an urban explorer, but it wasn't a remotely safe hobby. Cave-ins were not a rare occurrence. It was entirely possible to get so lost beneath Paris that you'd never be found.

TEN

"You're taking us in the wrong direction," Dorian said, craning his neck.

"This is the right way back to the apartment," I said as I pushed the wheelchair. In the apartment building that I wished hadn't been filled with such friendly tourists, who'd no doubt wish to greet and talk with my *grandmère* if they saw her.

"But I smell the *pain au levain*." Dorian's voice rose in excitement. "There is nothing like French bread, no?"

"I'll be sure to get some when I stop by the market this afternoon. Alone."

"Travel makes me so hungry," he said. "It will be faster if you buy bread and pastries now, and then return to the market. Are you not hungry as well?"

I was famished. But I nearly turned back when I saw the throng of people in line. Until I noticed the people weren't queuing to get into the bookshop or café, but the museum around the corner.

A vinyl banner swaying in the wind identified the Notre Dame exhibit. Affixed to stone columns with rope, the glossy materials looked out of place on the neoclassical building, even with an appropriate font and sepia color scheme. I hadn't realized that the museum with the illustration on display was so close—but I also hadn't counted on the line that snaked several blocks. How early did I need to show up, even with a ticket?

"Why are we stopping?" Dorian admonished. "We have not yet reached the patisserie." He gasped. "Are those people in line for pastries?"

"It looks like they're in line for the museum."

Dorian breathed a sigh of relief.

"That's bad," I said. "That means it'll be crowded, even with my ticket. I want to get a closer look at the charred illustration found at the cathedral without a throng of people around me."

He was silent for a moment. "You do not wish me to accompany you."

Of course I didn't. My plan was to get enough groceries to occupy Dorian for hours, leaving him in the apartment with both his pastries and a kitchen full of ingredients to cook us a nourishing meal. I hoped. It was one thing to use his disguise in an anonymous crowd, and another to be inspected going through security to enter the Victor Hugo exhibit.

"I didn't think it would be practical," I said, "so I only bought one ticket."

"I know."

"You know?"

"Yes. This is why I purchased my *own* ticket."

"Very funny." I'd been good at keeping my credit card safely hidden ever since a stand mixer costing several hundred dollars arrived on my front porch.

He had the audacity to giggle. "Your credit card number was very easy to memorize. Do humans have trouble with such a simple task?"

"But the security and the crowds," I blurted out. "They'll make things difficult and take a long time, and don't you want to stay in the safe, cozy apartment cooking—"

"You speak in a rush, as if you anticipate an argument."

"You don't object?"

"I bought a ticket *in case* it would prove practical. But as you said, the museum is so crowded. The night will be better."

I frowned. "That's for the *catacombs*, not the museum."

He shrugged so theatrically that I was worried his wings would push through the shawls.

"Dorian—"

"The more we argue on this street corner, Zoe Faust, the more attention you draw to us."

I gripped the wheelchair's handles so tightly I expected I'd get at least one blister. It was a good thing I had several healing salves with me.

"No breaking and entering."

He didn't answer.

"I'm serious, Dorian."

"I, too, am capable of serious thought. With my 'little gray cells,' I am *more* than capable of serious planning. I have assessed the situation and come up with the only plan that makes sense. I must steal the Lost Gargoyle of Paris before the backward alchemists can get to it themselves."

ELEVEN

I would have tossed Dorian from the wheelchair onto the street and had it out with him at that moment of idiocy if I hadn't known how much worse it would be for the gargoyle to be revealed to the world. Things had been so much easier before cell phones and CCTV cameras. I knew that was why he'd told me his plan in public. Which made me all the angrier.

Dorian has learned the not-so-subtle art of manipulating his scant few friends—by reminding us exactly of that fact. I knew it wasn't an easy life for him, always hiding from the world. That's why I gave in. A handful of people knew the real Dorian, but everyone else had only heard his voice, believing him to be a reclusive Frenchman who considered himself too disfigured to be seen in public. It was easier for him to pull off the con in the 1800s, when "unsightly" people were all too often hidden away. But now in the twenty-first century, some people thought I was the monster for enabling his hiding.

By the time we were back at the apartment, I'd calmed down enough that I no longer wanted to toss him off a balustrade. Barely.

With a large bag of pastries on Dorian's lap, from *éclairs* to *viennoiseries*, we made it through the courtyard and into the elevator of the apartment building without running into any other neighbors.

The rickety lift came to an abrupt and squeaky halt. I carefully stepped around the wheelchair to open the grate and check to make sure nobody else was in the hallway.

"We're alone," I said curtly.

Dorian bounded up the stairs to the attic apartment, leaving me to fold and carry the wheelchair. As soon as I shut the door behind us, he began unwrapping the shawls I'd bundled him in. He stepped on the edge of one of the scarves and spun around. "Ah, Zoe?" His voice was muffled. "Your assistance, *s'il vous plaît*?"

I had to bite my tongue to prevent myself from laughing. My impish friend had wrapped himself up like a rainbow mummy.

He sniffed. "Is your mockery called for?"

"Hold still." I tugged at the soft, tangled web of fabric.

"But I cannot move my wings!"

The more he squirmed, the more the cloth twisted around his folded wings. It took me several minutes to get him untangled.

"I told you the disguise of being your grandmother was a bad idea," he muttered as I tugged on his left horn.

"Earlier you said it was a great idea."

"I was merely being polite. There is no danger if people see me while I am in stone form." Freed from the confines of his disguise, he tucked his wings, squared his shoulders, and became completely still. As he did so, his gray skin hardened, and he was again stone.

I shivered. I knew he was fully aware even in this immobile, stone form. I knew I shouldn't have been worried, since he could transform himself back to life at will. But that hadn't always been the case. When he was desperate enough to seek out the help of a stranger—me—he'd been slowly reverting to stone. Alive. Awake. And trapped in stone.

"In stone form," I said to the immobile figure, shaking my worry away, "how would that work? A three-and-a-half-foot stone gargoyle on a scooter that I pushed around the city? Because that's certainly a great way to go unnoticed in the age of cell phone videos."

The stone began to vibrate. Dorian wriggled his horns, blinked his eyes, and came back to life. "Fair point. *Alors*… You have thought about my plan?"

"Yes, and it's still terrible."

"Where are you going? Is it to purchase food? You are walking to the wrong door."

"If these pipes work, I'm going to take a hot shower. I'll be more forgiving after working out some of the stiffness in my joints."

I emerged a few minutes later, having taken a long enough shower in the impossibly small bathroom to calm down before talking to the deceitful gargoyle. My stomach rumbled as I slipped into fresh clothes.

"Truce," I said to the gargoyle who was waiting impatiently. "Do you want to make a shopping list before I go to the market?"

"*Pft*. What do you think of me?" He scampered to the kitchen and grabbed a piece of paper from the counter.

"I can't carry fifty items. Do you want me to pick?"

He plucked the list from my hands and studied it with a critical eye.

While he studied his shopping list, I surveyed the tiny apartment. I hadn't taken time to fully explore the small space yet. I reached out to the small bookcase next to the couch and pulled a decade-old fashion magazine off the shelf. The owner certainly wasn't filling up her rental property by keeping entertainment materials up to date. With this location, I supposed she didn't need to. A handful of DVDs sat next to the old books and magazines, and an antique wooden box served as a bookend. Was it my imagination or was that an ouroboros carved on the lid? I reached my hand out to touch it, but before my fingers reached the box, Dorian slid a sheet of paper into my palm.

I smiled at the revised list of ingredients, my mind conjuring the feasts he'd create. It wasn't only a good plan to occupy Dorian, but it would let me recharge now and enable us to have a nourishing meal before exploring the catacombs that night. As an alchemist who's in tune with the planetary cycles, I'm rather useless after dark. I admit to succumbing to many of the conveniences of the twenty-first century, but in this case, it wasn't just a spoiled preference to wish to enjoy a good meal for dinner before we headed underground. I needed to be not only awake, but on high alert.

Dorian would never let me hear the end of it if I didn't shop at a proper farmers' market, and I agreed with him. Luckily it was early enough in the day that Marché Maubert would be open, so I took my limited supply of Euros, and left Dorian with the stack of outdated books in the apartment, hoping they would occupy him until he could get cooking.

I love the scent of French markets, above all else. The bounty isn't always as great as you'll find at farmers' markets back home in the U.S., and you won't always find the vegetable you're looking for, but everything is as fresh as can be. From the delicate strawberries with their sweet-tart aroma to the freshly baked sourdough rolls with their savory, yeasty scent, you know you're bringing home a treat. The young green garlic would be perfect with the freshly-picked crisp asparagus. Leeks and lemons, parsley and peas... I needed to stop before I had more than I could carry.

With one shoulder sagging from the bounty, I stopped by a shop for flour, oil, nuts, and the cleaning supplies Dorian needed for the oven. I was so weighed down with the ample supplies by the time I returned to the apartment, that I wasn't paying attention to my surroundings. It was stupid of me, but I hadn't been able to resist the produce and breads.

The courtyard of the apartment building packed a lot into a small amount of space. The calming tapping of water droplets from a Romanesque stone fountain set the mood for the tranquil garden. Angular hedges ran alongside the walkway, and four Noel des Champs apple trees provided shade over two wooden benches.

This time, I didn't make it to the door unnoticed. The handsome man who'd helped me with my bag was leaning against the fountain and swearing at his phone. But he smiled when he saw me.

"I never got your name." He pocketed his phone. "I'm Carter."

"Zoe." I gave him a friendly smile but kept walking.

"Zoe, who is always carrying a heavy load alone. Need help?"

"Groceries, I can handle."

"That's groceries in those bags? You're in Paris! You should be shopping for clothes and eating out."

"This *is* eating out. You can't get these exact foods and flavors at home."

"I never thought of it like that. Well, I hope you get out a bit, at least."

"I'm going to the Victor Hugo exhibit later."

"That's what I'm supposed to be doing in an hour, but my friend bailed on me."

"That explains the swearing at your phone."

He grimaced. "Sorry about that."

"I'm not a wilting flower. I've heard far worse."

"Then I'll have to do better next time. Hey, what time were you scheduled to go to the exhibit? I hear they're not always honoring the last set of tickets, if they haven't been able to get enough people through earlier."

"That can't be right. They have to honor our tickets."

"Not if it's a fire hazard. It's not like we're back home."

Now it was my turn to swear.

"Sorry, I didn't mean to be the bearer of theoretically possible bad news. If you're free in an hour you're welcome to have my extra ticket. My friend's not going to use it."

"One hour from now?"

The museum was already going to be crowded. It wouldn't hurt to have more company. Especially if I'd be closer to getting answers even sooner. Right?

TWELVE

Dorian was eagerly awaiting my return. Or rather, the return of bags full of food.

"I hope whatever you have in mind to cook for a late lunch can be done in half an hour," I said as he inspected the bags.

Dorian gasped.

"Did I forget something?" I frowned at the heavy bags.

"Your attitude. You are the one who insists transformations cannot be rushed."

"I have an opportunity to go to the museum at an earlier time slot. I promise I'll take lots of photos."

"And video," he added, not looking up from his bounty of vegetables.

"Yes. So with even more time at the museum than I previously thought, an illegal nocturnal visit definitely won't be necessary. Dorian? Are you paying attention?"

He looked up from behind a tangle of pea greens, tilted his head rather like a puppy dog, and blinked at me innocently. That was never a good sign.

"I am paying attention to the rich assortment of produce, bounty of nuts, and freshly ground flours. Never have I known someone who can select the highest quality—"

"You can stop the false flattery."

"It is not false—"

"It's a distraction."

"Many statements may contain two true elements at once."

I eyed Dorian as I arranged the fresh lavender in a salt-stained vase. "I haven't changed my mind. I'm not breaking in with you during the middle of the night." Now that I'd snacked on some of the fresh fruits at the market and was thinking with more clarity, something else occurred to me. "Why aren't you more interested in our trip to the catacombs?"

Dorian hadn't been with me when I'd explored the catacombs to rescue our friend earlier that year. He knew I'd discovered a secret alchemical laboratory below the cathedral, which although destroyed, could have been rebuilt.

"Don't you want to see if there's a need to steal the illustration before the backwards alchemists can steal it themselves?" I asked. "We need to see if they're back."

He gave a Gallic shrug and returned his attention to food. "This, *mon amie,* is more important." He sniffed the greens and nodded in satisfaction.

There was more to it, but he shrugged off my further questions as he sorted the groceries. Within a few minutes he'd cleaned the oven, readying it for a pan of chopped vegetables and a sheet-pan of ripped slices of bread. As the breadcrumbs and vegetables roasted, he expertly whisked a béchamel sauce in a stainless steel pot on the stovetop. We hadn't found a stepping stool in the apartment, so he was standing on top of the three largest books on the bookcase that we'd dusted off (a dictionary and encyclopedia from the 1970s and an even older textbook on French history), his clawed feet curled around the edges of the dusty *dictionnaire.*

I watched him cook, wondering what he was keeping from me. It couldn't be that he was simply distracted by cooking. Though I understood the sentiment as Dorian opened the oven and I was enveloped by the sweet scent of caramelizing vegetables. Fragrant leeks, green garlic, and asparagus filled one baking sheet, and the crisping breadcrumbs emitted an earthy scent. Donning an oven mitt, Dorian pulled each of the hot trays from the small oven and tossed them with an expert flick of his wrist that sent the contents several inches into the air before landing again on the baking sheet. He set the rickety plastic timer for five more minutes.

"You are still angry," Dorian said, stealing a glance at me before returning to his sauce of olive oil, flour, and oat milk.

"Do I have anything to be angry about?" He added a pinch of sea salt to the sauce. "If you're agreed that we're not stealing the Lost Gargoyle of Paris illustration, there's nothing for me to be angry about."

"*Bon*. Then we have nothing to fight about. You may set the table. Our late lunch will be done in a few minutes."

I took a bite of the caramelized vegetables slathered in the creamy sauce, with freshly toasted breadcrumbs and roasted walnuts sprinkled on top. The crisp, savory edges and the soft, sweet interior of the roasted vegetables struck the perfect balance, and the crunchy toppings brought an earthy deliciousness to round out the experience. It was a meal that provided the energy I needed to be fully aware of the security at the museum.

I added crushed peppermint leaves to my water bottle, donned my silver coat and hat, and left Dorian in the kitchen, where he was preparing for an afternoon of baking. I took the winding stairs instead of the elevator. The spiraling wooden handrail was well worn, but also well taken care of. The smooth surface was no longer even, but ebbed and flowed with the natural curves of where people needed a handhold as they traversed the uneven stairs.

Carter was already waiting by the fountain when I stepped outside. As he spotted me, he clutched his hand to his heart. "I'm not late, am I?"

"Early."

"You sure?" He studied my face. "Hell hath no fury like a woman scorned."

"Is my expression that grim?"

"Are you all right? That apartment seemed awfully dank. Are you sure it's good for your stay—"

"It's tiny but suits my needs. It must be the jet lag getting to me."

"I know just the cure for that," he said with a broad smile, meeting my gaze and holding it. "It's a gorgeous day. It'll be a lovely walk to the museum. But..." He glanced around the fountain.

A bee the size of my fingertip hovered around the flowers of the nearby tree. "The bee won't hurt you," I said.

"It's not that. I forgot something. Give me one minute. I need to grab my bag. I bought some designer souvenirs that turned out to be knock-offs. Can you believe that? I need to return them while I'm in that neighborhood." He grinned. "Back in a heartbeat."

It was a long heartbeat. More than five minutes later I was still standing in the beautiful courtyard. I wish I'd known I'd have time to call Max. It was now late enough that it was morning in Portland. I missed Max more than I thought I would after being away such a short time. It had been a long time since I'd been in love. Max Liu and I hadn't met under the most auspicious circumstances, and we didn't always see things the same way, but I knew he returned my feelings.

I sipped my mint tea and ran my fingers across the rough stone fountain. It was covered with more moss than I'd noticed earlier, and the faint trickle of water lulled me into believing a crowded twenty-first century city wasn't a few feet away.

"Ready to go." Carter appeared with a carry-on-size rolling bag. "I'm so sorry I kept you waiting so long. I never know where anything is when I'm traveling. I'm glad you waited for me."

"If I'd known you'd be so long, I would have called my boyfriend."

Carter held his free hand to his heart again. "I'm wounded. But I should have known. Yet the foolish man didn't come with you to Paris? Are you sure he's a keeper?"

"As sure as I am that you're a shameless flirt."

"Ha. Well, that explains your bad mood. You miss him, don't you?"

"Of course I miss him."

"I'll take it as my moral duty to cheer you up. Because I'm a *harmless* shameless flirt. Tell me about Oregon."

"That obvious?"

"Elementary, my dear Zoe. Your cute boots are high quality faux leather, you have a Powell's Books sticker on your stainless-steel water bottle, and you dye your hair in a trendy yet laid-back style."

I paused and picked a daffodil growing from a crack in the sidewalk. "That Powell's sticker was next to two National Parks stickers, so why not guess I'm from Utah or Arizona?"

"I'm great at reading people. Or... I could also admit that I spotted the PDX airport tag on your bag when I carried it up the stairs."

I groaned and we both laughed.

"In all honesty, I don't know that I'd have been as gallant if I'd known your luggage was filled with hardback books. That's what was inside, wasn't it? I wish I'd met you in the States. I could have told you there are plenty of English-language books in France."

"Good to know for next time."

"Great craft beer in Portland," he said. "But here? I'm in love with the wine. There are some great bars—referred to as cafés here, you know—on this street. You picked a great building. Every apartment on this side of the complex that's above the ground floor—that's what they call the first floor here—has a view of Notre Dame. It's such a shame about the fire."

True to his word, Carter flirted the whole way. He was quite good at being charming, and I appreciated the distraction, wondering what I'd find at the exhibit. But I missed Max and wished he'd been my company instead.

The long line I'd seen earlier outside the Museum of Parisian History had died down, and we reached the ticket counter after waiting for only ten minutes. I was pleased to see three lines with security guards who were searching visitors, and turnstiles we had to walk through before entering the museum. Marcel Boucher was right that they were taking security seriously.

"Your valise, sir." The security guard indicated Carter's bag. He hefted it onto the table and the guard zipped it open and inspected the silk scarves.

"Souvenirs for friends back home," Carter said to her.

She zipped the bag and pointed to the coat check station. "You'll need to check the valise."

"Really? It's not that big."

"I'm sorry, sir." She gestured again toward the coat check area again.

"Unbelievable," he muttered to me. "Did you see that? She wrinkled those scarves on purpose—who knows if I'll be able to return them now. And I can't take my bag inside? If this were the States—"

"We're holding up the line," I said. "Why don't you just check the bag?" I was surprised he hadn't tried to charm the guard.

He grinned sheepishly. "You're right. We don't want to miss the star of the show. A long-missing drawing by Victor Hugo himself. I hear it's going to be auctioned off for millions once this exhibit ends."

THIRTEEN

Before I had a chance to ask Carter more about where he'd heard that outrageous figure, we were ushered into a dark room. In the crowd and relative darkness, I lost him immediately.

The room wasn't entirely devoid of light. The square, high-ceilinged room was fitted with overhead lighting only at the edges, which pointed toward the display on the walls. For a moment, I forgot all about the supposed Victor Hugo illustration and stonemason's journal. I was transported to another time. Or rather, a range of times that spanned the past.

Instead of artwork or other historical objects, a mural stretched across the walls showing the timeline of the history of Notre Dame. Along with a true timeline with dates and text along a thick black line that circled the room, an artist had used subdued colors to tell the story of the cathedral visually.

The first date was in the twelfth century. The cornerstone of Notre Dame de Paris — Our Lady of Paris — was laid in 1163. The original architectural records were lost long ago, but we know generations of workers spent their lives laboring at the site and never saw its completion. The finishing touches of the cathedral were put in place nearly 200 years later, in 1345.

Notre Dame Cathedral cost about $1 billion in today's dollars to build. A 3-D video played next to the first date on the timeline, showing how the stones were built up, and how new technology had advanced to make it possible to build taller buildings with thinner walls that could also accommodate the huge stained-glass windows. A lot of new, experimental features were being forged with Notre Dame. Yet still, the weight was underestimated, so stress fractures. The solution was flying buttresses, arches braced into the walls, which Notre Dame was one of the first cathedrals to use.

The timeline went on, showing the kings and their successors who presided over the construction over many generations and wars. Through the Hundred Years War, work on the cathedral continued. Henry VI of England was crowned King of France in the cathedral; he was ten years old.

In addition to Catholic masses and ceremonies of state, it was also the site of executions. The last of the Knights Templar was burned at the stake in the courtyard in 1314. Numerous restorations over the centuries kept the cathedral structurally sound and as a thriving church, before the French Revolution of 1798, when the cathedral briefly became a temple of reason.

By the time Victor Hugo wrote his novel, much of the cathedral was a wreck, with purposeful destruction that included beheading the prominent stone statues of kings, until the cathedral's savior appeared in the 1830s. That savior had an unexpected face. A bohemian artist and writer who was active not in the church but in the politics of the day.

Victor Hugo's *Notre-Dame de Paris* was published in 1831. The Gothic novel inspired the public, capturing their imaginations and filling their souls with French pride. The novel imagined the cathedral as it was in the Middle Ages. Quasimodo, the tragic bell-ringer at the heart of the novel, rang the bells of the cathedral to let Parisians know when to wake up, when their day of labor was over, and when to attend church. That much reflected life in the Middle Ages compared to the nineteenth century.

Quasimodo also lived among a wide array of gargoyles in the cathedral—most of which didn't exist when the novel was written. Far more Gothic creatures were sprinkled throughout the story than existed in reality.

Thus most of Victor Hugo's depiction *wasn't* what the cathedral looked like in the Middle Ages. That's what had been misrepresented in the illustration of the cathedral on the billboard in the airport as well. The gallery of gargoyles that throngs of visitors climbed hundreds of steps to visit, up until the fire, fit so perfectly into the ethos of Middle Ages that it was easy to assume that's the period of time from which they'd sprung. I was glad to see the exhibit educated viewers with the true history.

The timeline ended with the last years of the previous century, with the 800th anniversary celebrated in 1963, and a minor restoration in the 1990s that addressed the damage pollution had done to the stone.

Even though I knew much of the history already, the visual timeline was so engaging that I kept forgetting to look for ways an alchemist who wasn't pure of heart might think to get inside.

The doors leading into and out of the room were solid, but there were other ways into a room.

As above, so below.

That was one of the core principles of alchemists.

The hardwood floor under my boots was solid and didn't creak under the weight of the hundred people in the room. There were no skylights in the high ceiling, but there were two vents, both of which would be large enough for a small-boned person to fit through.

A docent tried valiantly to keep me moving, since they'd packed more people in than was safe, and many more people were behind me. I let her usher me onward. I'd seen what I needed to.

In the next room, the newly discovered prized drawing took center stage. I closed my eyes for a moment and breathed in the scent of old paper. Unlike the previous room, this one felt old. I could feel the history. To be more accurate, I smelled it. Even though the original documents were behind glass, I sensed the smokiness of charcoal, the crisp scent of vellum, and the earthy aroma of leather.

I was relieved to see the Lost Gargoyle of Paris behind a thick case of glass in the center of the room. The slim leather journal next to the illustration, in the same glass case.

The museum wasn't taking any chances with security. In addition to the two security guards who flanked the two exits of the room, the cube that protected the illustration and journal was constructed of glass that looked way too thick to smash, and screws thicker than my fingers bolted the glass to a pedestal below.

Even Alkahest, the universal solvent, wouldn't dissolve glass.

I couldn't tell if the glass case was alarmed, but I spotted two security cameras pointing at it from different sides of the room. I looked away from them quickly, turning my attention back to the Lost Gargoyle of Paris.

Victor Hugo's black pen-and-ink wash showed his skilled, sure hand. The rendering of the gargoyle showed not only the details of the unique horns and wings, but also proportions noted in charcoal pencil.

Carter's information about the auction was correct. The placard underneath the illustration explained that it would be on display for a month before being auctioned off, with the proceeds given to the fund to rebuild Notre Dame cathedral.

Since the illustration had been found stuck inside a workman's journal, there had been initial confusion about ownership. It was quickly cleared up when a descendant of the stonemason who lived in Paris said the family wanted to donate the illustration to the restoration. Madame Orleans was an artist herself, so she loved the idea of donating a piece of art that could help restore the cathedral.

A tall man with pointy elbows jostled me out of the way to get a better look at the illustration. I didn't mind. I was more interested in the journal with the ourobouros on the cover. I wondered why I'd felt something was wrong with this discovery in the first place. Though I couldn't look inside the journal or handle it, it felt like something from the 1850s. And I knew that many of Viollet-le-Duc's drawings had come to light because of a similar discovery tucked inside the pages of an old journal, when the elderly granddaughter of one of the original stone carvers had gone through an old family box and discovered the forgotten treasures, now on display at another Parisian museum.

In this more brightly lit room, Carter found me as I was taking a surreptitious video.

"You're a naughty one," he whispered in my ear.

"Are you going to confiscate my phone?"

"Only to add my phone number, if I've charmed you to sufficiently to pretend your boyfriend doesn't exist for the duration of your stay in Paris. No? In that case I'll let you keep it." He moved abruptly to the other side of me. "And I'm going to shield you from the line of sight of that guard."

"Thanks."

"Just be sure to tag me if you become Instagram famous for your photos."

"All done." I slipped the phone back into my bag.

"I don't get it, do you?" he said in a conspiratorial whisper. "All this fuss over a sketch on a piece of paper?"

Carter left before me, bored with the exhibit and saying he was going to at least try to return the scarves and needed to buy wine for the apartment courtyard sunset gathering.

I stopped at a bookshop to buy a few books to entertain Dorian while he was cooped up in the apartment, since I doubted the old reading materials in the apartment would keep him occupied. He might actually have read the old French dictionary he was using as a stepping stool, but he was verbose enough as it was. I didn't need him getting more ideas.

When I arrived back at the apartment, I didn't see the gargoyle. I'd expected him to greet me immediately, eager for news of the illustration.

"Dorian?"

Two gray horns appeared over the back of the tiny sofa, followed by an expanse of wings and the scowling face of a gargoyle. Like Quasimodo, he was used to hiding.

"We have been burglarized," he declared.

Chapter 14

"Burglarized?" I rushed to my backpack. I breathed deeply, thinking through the items I'd brought with me. It's not like I traveled with a journal of my alchemical experiments, but had I taken anything else that could expose me?

Dorian climbed out from behind the sofa and sat down. "This is what happens when you do not take me with you."

"They saw you?"

"Of course not," he huffed indignantly. "I hid behind the sofa."

"Good." I reached for my backpack. "I don't see anything missing from my bag."

"Your bag was not touched."

"What did the burglar take, then?" I looked around the apartment. I hadn't committed it to memory, but nothing seemed amiss, aside from the bookshelf where the books had been knocked over. The box being used as a bookend must have fallen under the couch when Dorian hurried to his hiding place. With how much dust there was in the apartment, I'd worry about retrieving it later.

"Nothing."

I studied the gargoyle. "Why did you call him a burglar?"

"*Her*. A woman let herself into the apartment. She was dressed in elegant black but wore hideous sneakers. No respectable Frenchwoman—"

I groaned. "A woman. Wearing comfortable clothing. Who didn't break the door open. And who didn't take any of our belongings?"

"*Oui*. This is what I said." He raised his voice. "Do you need a tincture to clean out your ears? Are they clogged from the altitude of the—"

"I heard you perfectly. I heard you describing a cleaning lady."

"She did not clean! She was nervous and left within minutes."

"Because she sensed the eyes of a gargoyle watching her."

"Ah, so." He scratched his chin, looking very much like gargoyle in the illustration I'd just seen. "I have always wondered how it is that people sense they are being watched. Science has not come up with a rational explanation for this, yet it is true, *non*?"

"Yes," I agreed as my heart rate began to return to normal. "And I need to contact the landlord to let her know we don't need cleaning services."

I sent the property manager a message right away. As soon as I hit "send," I looked up and saw Dorian staring at me apprehensively.

"Now, what news have you from the exhibit?" he asked. "What of the security?"

"Dorian."

He widened his large black eyes. "You think ill of my intentions? I am attempting to help! I think only of how difficult it will be for us to protect the illustration from the bad alchemists."

I wasn't fooled by his well-practiced innocent expression. I pressed play on the video I'd taken on my phone.

"D'accord," he mumbled, watching the screen intently. He asked me to scroll through the photos and play the video three more times before beginning to cook dinner—a plant-based version of bolognaise sauce using the fresh tomatoes and extra carrots (which he insisted would not only add a hearty texture but help our night vision) to accompany homemade pasta made possible by the rolling pin he found tucked into a small kitchen drawer.

He was uncharacteristically silent as he cooked. I didn't mind. I was still thinking about what I was missing. *As above, so below.* Did the catacombs stretch beneath the museum?

"Dinner will be served in five minutes," Dorian said, startling me from my thoughts.

"Oh! You've invented a new shape of pasta."

"It is not my desire," he huffed. "This rolling pin proved quite uneven."

I stifled a laugh.

"You believe this gargoyle drawn by Victor Hugo resembles me?" He stood tall on the *dictionnaire* and wriggled his horns.

"Is that why you've been acting strangely? Because you worry about being in the spotlight?"

"I was the original *Penseur*. It is my nature to be contemplative, no?"

#

After dinner, Dorian held up one of the DVDs I'd seen on the shelf. It was the cartoon version of *The Hunchback of Notre Dame* which I'd seen among the entertainment options the property manager had provided.

"You've never seen it?" I asked.

"How would I have seen it? Before I met you, I worked as a companion for blind people."

"Do you want to watch it tonight after dinner? I'll want help staying up before we explore the catacombs."

He eyed the cover of the DVD skeptically. "These gargoyles… They do not appear terribly dignified."

As the movie progressed, he gaped at the screen more and more frequently. "But these gargoyle friends of Quasimodo in this cartoon have no legs! They must *hop*. Hop! Such indignity. I was led to believe the animated version of the novel was not a tragedy. *Quelle horreur*."

As Dorian spoke, his gray form grew fuzzy before my eyes. My eyes couldn't stay focused. The later it became, the more my energy cycled out of me.

"Zoe? Are you aware you are lying down on the divan?"

"I'm only resting my eyes for a moment."

"This is not good. It is not yet late enough. "

"Wake me in an hour."

#

I hadn't been asleep long when I sat up with a jolt. In the darkness, my heart thudded in my chest. What had woken me?

I stirred and moved my stiff neck. I looked around in the shadows of nearly complete darkness. "What's happening?" I asked Dorian. I knew he'd be awake. He didn't sleep.

No answer.

"Dorian?"

I scrambled out of bed and found the switch of the bedside lamp. The solitary window of the apartment was ajar.

I pushed the window open further and looked out.

"Dorian?" I called again, my spirits falling.

"Oh, Dorian," I whispered to myself. "What have you done?"

I searched every inch of the apartment, including inside the oven and fridge. It was as I feared. The gargoyle was gone.

FIFTEEN

"The other statues, those of monsters and demons, had no hatred for him – he resembled them too closely for that. It was rather the rest of mankind that they jeered at. The saints were his friends and blessed him; the monsters were his friends and kept watch over him."

— Victor Hugo, Notre-Dame de Paris

This was a complication he hadn't seen coming. *Why was Zoe Faust really here?*

He couldn't let her interfere with his plan.

The Museum of Parisian History was usually overshadowed by the bigger museums of Paris, but the small, private museum was in the limelight since they had been nimble enough to pull together a winning proposal for the exhibit. It was officially called *L'Histoire de Notre-Dame*, but everyone was calling it the Victor Hugo exhibit featuring his Lost Gargoyle of Paris illustration.

The illustration was perfect. Powerful. It captured the spirit of the cathedral.

Regardless of the added risk, he would move forward as planned.

SIXTEEN

I pulled on a long sweater over leggings, and slipped on my boots and silver raincoat, before rushing down the winding staircase. The soles of my boots echoed in the stairwell, overlapping with my heart thudding in my ears.

Several eyes turned toward me as I skidded into the courtyard. It was just past 11 o'clock, and half a dozen young tourists were still gathered around the fountain sipping wine.

"Join us, Zelda!" Carter called out when he saw me. His arm was draped over his friend's shoulder, and his words were slurred. "Naughty girl. You said you had other plans." He swore. "Sorry, I messed up your name, didn't I? Zena?"

"Did you see… um… anything strange?"

"Like what?"

"Maybe…" what could I say? "Like a cat burglar?"

"Someone's a true crime buff, eh?" a woman with an Australian accent giggled.

#

I ran toward the museum Dorian had threatened to rob.

As I reached the street with the museum, the shrill bleating of an alarm sounded.

The museum was now in my line of sight. I kept running. I reached the front of the museum at the same time as several others who'd been having a drink at the bar on the same block.

"*Que se passe-t'il*?" I asked above the blaring alarm.

Shrugs. Shakes of heads. Nobody knew what was happening. I gasped as the front doors of the museum burst open.

A man dressed in the uniform of a security guard ran toward us, a phone gripped in his right hand, and his left hand balled into a fist. "*Où est allé le voleur?*"

"Nobody besides you came out," a large man answered in French.

"That's impossible." The guard spat out the words. "The other exit is secured. They must have come back out this way."

A chorus of "no's" followed, and his frown grew deeper.

"You said *they*," I said. "You saw them?"

He looked down at his nose at me. I'm not a small woman, yet he towered over me. "The thieves," he answered. "It must have been multiple people. How else could they have done this so quickly?"

"What did they steal?" My heart pulsed in my neck and my mouth went dry as I asked the question. I didn't want to know the answer. As it happened, I didn't get one. The guard didn't demean himself to answer me.

The sound of sirens competed with the alarm, and a moment later two police cars pulled up. I watched as two officers spoke to the guard, two others searched for the thieves, and three more vehicles with sirens pulled up. The alarm was still sounding and my head was beginning to throb.

By this time, a crowd of at least 50 people had gathered. Two young officers were attempting to usher people behind the waist-high metal barricades they were efficiently putting in place.

The scents of musty mist, wine, and cigarettes hung in the air. Everyone apart from me was dressed more appropriately for both the chill of the evening air and the elegance of the city. It was early enough in the night that many people had still been out, or at least awake.

As the crowd grew, I stayed as close as I could.

An officer loudly chastised a petite woman in bright pink running shoes when she disregarded the request for the public to move beyond the barricade. She ignored him and continued filming the police and security guards who were conferring at the entrance to the museum. She didn't stop filming as an officer twice her size wrapped his arm around her waist and physically removed her. Her body really was quite tiny, but not her voice. The officer carried her effortlessly, while listening stoically to her animated protests. I'd thought I was up on the latest swearwords in French. Apparently I was mistaken.

"*Ça m'est égal,*" he said, unceremoniously lifting her over the barricade.

She made a rude gesture at his back and looked as if she might be getting ready to jump over the fencing, until she caught me watching her escapade. She smiled mischievously and made her way over to me instead.

"*Tout va bien*?" I asked her. Nobody else had.

She paused a moment before replying, and when she did it was in French-accented English. "You're not French, are you?"

I winced. I was getting rusty. I shook my head.

"Your accent is very good."

"Did you learn any more than I did about what's happening?" I asked.

"You've been here a while too?"

"I came quickly when I heard all the noise," I said cautiously, not wanting to reveal I'd been there before the alarm had sounded.

She nodded. Any remaining excitement from having crossed a police line was now gone, replaced by indignant anger. "The famous Victor Hugo illustration has been stolen."

It was as I feared.

Dorian. What had he done?

The woman kept talking, explaining that she'd been out for a run along the Seine before bed and been curious so she followed the sirens, but I was barely listening until she said, "It was such a strange story the police were insisting on, so I began to film them."

"Strange?" I echoed, fearful that she was about to say the thief was a gargoyle.

"Thieves got inside," she said, "only… the odd thing is that what the guard and police are saying is impossible."

"Why impossible?"

"Because the museum has an alarm system that *wasn't* deactivated. The alarm rang, as it should have, but when the security team arrived in under a minute, the illustration was already gone."

That was exactly my impression, and also explained why the guard was so angry. There was no way anyone had time to get in and out.

Dorian was a master at picking locks. Not only did a talented magician raise him, but his stone claws served him well as lock-picks.

"The illustration was behind that thick glass case," I murmured. "With all those bolts."

"You've been," she said. "It's impressive, isn't it? So is the security. The security guards were telling the police the only way to open it was to unscrew all of the massive bolts. The burglars didn't smash the case. The cameras went dark, and the thieves unscrewed all the bolts *and* put them back. Yet the case inside was empty."

"In less than a minute?" I repeated.

She nodded. "I told you. Impossible."

One minute. Even Dorian couldn't have achieved such a feat.

"I wonder if I can sell this video to the press," she mused. The mischievous glimmer in her eye was back. "*Bonsoir.*"

The Victor Hugo illustration was gone, yet it was impossible for it to have vanished.

As I was taking that in, an animated voice rose over the commotion. A voice I recognized. Professor Boucher.

"*C'est elle!*" He pointed in my direction. "That woman knows something about the theft!"

I ran.

SEVENTEEN

I was lucky the crowd had grown so large, and that Marcel Boucher had opted for theatrics instead of quietly alerting the police to my presence.

What was he doing there anyway?

I slipped away from the crowd unseen, and kept running until I found a small courtyard with an oak tree large enough for me to hide behind. I leaned against its gnarled trunk, closed my eyes, and caught my breath.

How could Dorian have done this? And how does one find a gargoyle who's on the lam in a city he knows better than you?

"Zoe?"

I froze.

"Zoe, is that you?"

The voice wasn't that of Marcel Boucher's. Or that of anyone I recognized.

"What are you running from?" a second voice asked.

Neither of the voices sounded like police officers there to arrest me. It wasn't the friendly tone. I wasn't naive enough to think the police wouldn't lull me into a false sense of security. It was the age of the two women who spoke. They were young voices. I would have sworn they were the voices of teenagers.

I peeked out from behind the tree and saw two young women, who didn't look much older than their teens, if that, approaching me.

"I thought that might be you," the taller woman said in French. "We have a mutual friend."

"Dorian?"

She raised an eyebrow and looked at her friend. "I told you it was her. Now we don't have to call her."

My head throbbed. I was no good at night. I was out of my element and badly needed to recharge, but I had to focus and navigate the precarious situation of asking two French teenagers how they happened to know a living gargoyle.

"Um, how do you know Dorian?" I asked.

"He wants you to know he didn't do it," the other woman said. "But he intends to find out who did."

They introduced themselves as Lakshmi and Alix. They were university students who were having a drink with friends at the bar down the street when they saw someone dressed in a costume running down the alley next to the bar.

Both Alix and Lakshmi were into the cosplay scene and loved attending conventions, so they followed him, disappointed because they thought they'd missed one happening that week.

When they caught up with him, they saw he was dressed as a famous gargoyle of Notre Dame, and thought he was part of the publicity to raise money for the cathedral.

"I thought our angel and demon costumes were good," Lakshmi said, "but Dorian's costume is one of the best we've ever seen. Do you know if he made it himself? I couldn't tell if he was shy or selfish, if he didn't want us to steal his costume designer source."

"He rarely tells me everything either. He asked you to find me?"

"Dorian is a character," Lakshmi said. "He said you'd accuse him of this museum robbery. He swears he didn't do it. But he didn't want you to worry that he might not come home tonight."

I groaned.

"You two are way more into role playing than we are," Alix said.

EIGHTEEN

An hour later, I wouldn't say I was *wide* awake, but I was too frustrated to sleep. I didn't know what I was up against. An art historian—and possibly now the police—thought I had something to do with the theft of the Lost Gargoyle of Paris from an impenetrable museum. And my best friend might have been the one who did. Regardless of who'd done it, they'd pulled off an impossible heist.

So of course I couldn't sleep and instead proceeded with my plan to find the alchemy lab in the catacombs.

I dressed in dark gray slacks, a black turtleneck under my silver coat, sturdy boots, and took two flashlights. I hesitated at the door of my apartment and closed my eyes, resting my forehead on the heavy door. I wasn't totally confident it was the right decision to go without Dorian. I can die just as easily as anyone else.

Alchemy doesn't grant eternal life. Alchemists who've discovered the Elixir of Life can still be killed. We simply don't age. At least most of us don't. As for me, *most of me* didn't age. I must have gotten something wrong, just like I always do when I try to make gold, because every hair on my body turned white as time went by. Yet the rest of me stayed trapped in the body of a 28-year-old. Which is both a blessing and a curse.

Even though I think of myself as an accidental alchemist, that's not entirely accurate. I knew what I was getting myself into. I didn't choose the path for myself, but I gladly accepted it. I was desperately seeking the Elixir of

Life to save my brother's life. My efforts didn't pay off in time to save him, and the guilt took a long time to get over. It was only recently, with friends I loved dearly, that I felt like I might be fully healed. Which is why Dorian's betrayal felt all the more raw.

I found the metal grate that led into the secret entrance to the catacombs, and eased myself into the darkness.

Grasping one of the flashlights, and using the map I'd been given earlier that year, I made my way from the tunnels strewn with empty plastic water bottles and cigarette butts to the lesser-known tunnels that only the most hardcore urban explorers knew.

The walls were rough and the air was stale and metallic. The mineral content made the air feel heavy. After another ten minutes of walking on rough surfaces, I reached what at first glance appeared to be a dead end. This was where my map ended. Beyond lay the secret entrance to the backward alchemy lab.

The dead end was an optical illusion. I shone my light at the ground to find the opening. An overlapping wall disguised a two-foot gap that fed into a continuing tunnel. I stepped through, and the metallic scent grew stronger. This was it. I was on the right path to the alchemy lab.

The narrow tunnel gave way to a room with a high-vaulted ceiling. I hated to call this an alchemy lab. Even before it was destroyed, it had lacked the glass vessels, books, and assorted ingredients that true alchemists used. Instead, this was a dilletante's man-cave. Next to a comfy, well-used armchair was a single table for alchemical processes. The table for actual work had barely been used.

Inside the space that should have been sacred, there was no evidence the backward alchemists had returned. There were no smells associated with any alchemical process, no matter how small. And no scent of the fire from Notre Dame above. But I was far from relieved.

It appeared that backward alchemists *weren't* back. If Dorian had somehow pulled off the impossible and stolen the illustration, he'd done it for nothing.

NINETEEN

"His cathedral was enough for him. It was peopled with marble figures of kings, saints and bishops who at least did not laugh in his face and looked at him with only tranquility and benevolence."
– Victor Hugo, Notre-Dame de Paris

He'd been bullied as a child. Not many people knew that. They wouldn't laugh at him now. Not with his most brilliant plan yet.

He looked at the illustration that would make him a very rich man. The gargoyle looked back at him, seeming almost alive. It was eerie how well talented artists could make beasts come alive. He couldn't suppress a smile.

Who was he kidding? Why would he even try to suppress his smile? He grinned, took one last look at the charred sketch, and placed it inside the antique, velvet-lined box with the alchemical image carved into its wooden lid.

TWENTY

I woke up in the morning to the scent of stewed fruit and bubbling dough.

I'd been dreaming of Max, walking hand in hand through a forest of trees that became a forest of arched wooden beams. As the trees transformed into the man-made structure, in that surreal way that dreams possess no time, our fingertips slipped slowly apart long after I lost sight of him. I'd called him before going to sleep, when I got back to the empty apartment shortly after midnight. I caught him while he was eating lunch. He happily set aside his bowl of bibimbop (from a Portland food truck) to talk. In spite of my apprehension about where Dorian was, talking with Max had calmed me down, and at some point in the night I fell into a restless sleep.

I sat up and stretched my tense shoulders.

Dorian handed me a plate with two crêpes. "As much as I wished to, I am not the heroic soul who stole the illustration. Crêpe?"

"Lakshmi and Alix told me you'd say that." I set the plate down and went to the sink for a glass of water.

"*Bon*. I thought you would prefer I give them your number than worrying about me if you woke up and found me gone."

"You left the window open. Dorian, how could you?"

"I swear to you, *mon amie*, I am not lying. I did not steal the illustration."

"Even if I believe you—which remains to be seen—you know better than to go out while so many people are awake."

"But Zoe, I have learned of cosplay! It is short for 'costume play' and many young people from all across the world dress up in life-like costumes. They believed me to be a short man wearing a costume. They were most impressed by my wings." He unfolded his gray wings a few inches. The feather-like wings weren't exactly like the feathers of any bird, nor were they like the wings of a bat. They were uniquely gargoyle. And uniquely born of the sandstone of the Seine and Notre Dame cathedral.

"You know the danger—"

"They showed me photographs of their own costumes," Dorian said, "and those of others. These are far more than Halloween costumes. They *become* their characters. Lakshmi and Alix dress as an angel and demon who are in love. They laughed and spoke of dancing on the head of a pin—I did not know what that meant, but they were charming young ladies."

"You really didn't have anything to do with the theft?"

"Not even as a witness." He looked up at me with his most innocent expression, with his horns bending over. "I was attempting to be heroic. Like the gallant Quasimodo. I wished to guard against the backward alchemists, to hold vigil while a certain unnamed alchemist—whose name rhymes with Snowy Joust—*napped,* I might add. I hid as a stone gargoyle on the rafters of the mansion housing the museum, wishing to hear what had transpired. Then I heard the alarm, followed by sirens."

"And the illustration disappeared from within a locked glass case."

Dorian's black eyes grew wide. "I understand why they thought you a witch."

"I woke up and didn't find you here. I knew where you must have gone. I got close before they installed the barricades."

"Barricades. *Pfft.* We French have a proud history of protest. *Les flics* are so quick to use their inegalitarian barricades, as if those flimsy fences could stop us if we wanted to—"

"Dorian."

He cleared his throat. "Yes. You were saying you heard of this impossible disappearance as well."

"I saw it as well. There wasn't time for anyone to have gotten out through the front door. There must be another way out." I thought back to what I'd seen inside. I didn't like the rude guard, so I would have liked it to be an inside job, but he was far too large to fit through the vents in the ceiling.

"There was no other way out," Dorian said.

"Unless they came from above or below."

"Said like an alchemist. But no, both possibilities are impossible. Below the floorboards are solid concrete. The air vents are not even large enough for a small child. Or a gargoyle, I might add, if a certain alchemist is still suspicious of a goodhearted chimera."

"How do you know all this?"

"I overheard *les flics*. Yet I learned no more. Once more people gathered, I thought it prudent to move, so I climbed down and went in search of a perch across the street. This is where Lakshmi and Alix found me. They asked what 'con' I was attending. They were persistent and followed me into the alley, asking to get a better look at my impeccable costume." He squared his shoulders and puffed up his wings. "Are you ready for your crêpes?"

"I'm ready for you to tell me what you did for the rest of the night."

"But they will get cold."

I accepted the plate.

"*Bon.*"

"I'll eat if you keep talking."

But Dorian was silent as I took a bite of the darker buckwheat crêpe. The melted chocolate on the inside exploded with flavor in my mouth. Bittersweet chocolate with a hint of sweetness and spice from cardamom.

"You only get away with ignoring what I asked you because this is so good." I took another bite.

"I know I am bucking tradition adding a sweet rather than savory filling to buckwheat." Dorian grinned and pointed at the other crêpe. "Now try this one."

"I don't need two crêpes for breakfast."

"A taste test," he said. "You will confirm who is the better chef. One is from a famous Parisian baker, the other is freshly made by your humble friend—"

"You're kidding." I set the plate down more forcefully than I'd intended. The fork clattered to the floor.

"You doubt that I could create such a delectable crêpe? Your lack of faith wounds me."

"With your new-found confidence in your 'disguise' you went to a bakery on your own this morning?"

"I am not so careless, Zoe. Alix works part time at a patisserie. She had a delivery service bring an assortment of pastries. I promised her I'd return the favor before we left. Here. Let me get you another fork."

"I'm only going to taste the second crêpe if you first tell me what exactly you were doing last night."

"And then you will reciprocate."

"I'll go first, because my story is the quickest. The backward alchemists haven't returned. I went to the catacombs and their secret alchemy lab is untouched."

Dorian frowned but didn't look surprised.

"Now you," I said.

He handed me a fork in desperate need of polishing. "I was using my little gray cells."

"What did you discover?"

He gave me a sad smile. "First, that Paris is no longer my home. I love so many things about this city, yet... I miss Portland."

Why did he make it so difficult to stay mad at him? "I know the feeling."

"It is good that we can go home soon."

"You mean now that the illustration is gone and we've failed in our mission?"

"No. We must destroy the illustration."

I choked on the second crêpe. Which, to give Dorian full credit, wasn't as good as the one he'd made. "To keep it from the alchemists I told you aren't here? You admit you *did* take it?"

"No. I know who did."

TWENTY-ONE

Was Dorian serious that he knew who'd accomplished the impossible theft?

"Who?"

"Your boyfriend."

"Max? I know you have some issues with Max, but—"

"Not *that* boyfriend." He rolled his eyes. "Your suitor here in Paris."

My suitor? "Carter? He's the one person I know couldn't possibly have taken it. He was here in the apartment building courtyard all night. With about a dozen witnesses."

Dorian frowned. "*C'est impossible.*"

"It's not only possible, but I saw it with my own eyes. I saw him moments before the alarm."

"But I saw him...." He gasped. "I have solved it!" He paused and raised a clawed finger for dramatic effect. "Carter the criminal must have a twin. They are criminal masterminds, because nobody knows they are twins—"

"Dorian. I know you've been reading a lot of Gothic fiction lately, but we have no reason to believe Carter has a twin. Or that he's the thief. What do you think you saw him do?"

"He had the pen-and-ink illustration. I saw him through his window, directly below ours, when I was crawling back to our window early this morning, an hour before sunrise."

"You mean the illustration with replicas being sold at the gift shop of the museum I visited with him this afternoon?"

Dorian frowned so deeply I was afraid his chin might chip off. "Why, then, was he gloating over it in the middle of the night?"

"Because he's a happy drunk and couldn't sleep, I expect. He was so drunk at the time of the theft he didn't even remember my name. That takes a while to recover from."

"Yet—" Dorian broke off, clasped his hands behind his back, and began to pace. "Why was he gloating?"

That gave me pause. But it still didn't make sense. "The coincidence of us being in the same building as the thief? The implausibility of Carter having a perfect alibi that can only be solved by the existence of a twin? No, I don't buy it. A lot of people have gargoyle illustrations. Your brethren are popular."

"Especially amongst thieves who have stolen them," Dorian huffed.

"Or gargoyles who are trying to cast suspicion away from themselves."

Dorian's mouth fell open. "You continue to consider me a suspect?"

"No. I believe you would have done it if you could, but even with your claws you couldn't have opened that case in the short amount of time. Nobody could have."

His eyes narrowed. "My father taught me well. I could have done it." I could see it in his eyes as it dawned on him what he'd admitted. He sputtered, "Yet I did not!"

"There's more going on here that we're missing. I talked to people at the scene and read the news reports when I got back last night. There's conflicting information, as there always is, but one thing is certain. There wasn't time for *anyone* to have stolen the illustration."

"Unless your boyfriend removed the illustration earlier, replaced it with flash paper that would consume itself at a later time—"

"Stop calling him that. Although that's not a bad idea."

"Dorian Robert-Houdin never has a bad idea."

"Two words," I said. "Tarragon chocolate."

"She remembers the one failed experiment in all my years as a chef."

"What you're right about is that we're definitely missing something related to how the theft was accomplished. It wasn't flash paper, though. There was no way anyone could have stolen the illustration while the museum was open. I saw how secure it was. But it's impossible for it to have been impossible." I groaned at my choice of words. And I had no excuse. It was morning, when my body had the most clarity. It was the situation that was muddled.

"Hang on," I added, another issue belatedly catching up with me. "Why do you want to destroy the illustration? You don't believe me about the backward alchemists not having returned?"

"Those lazy alchemists were never the main concern of mine."

There are moments in life when part of you realizes what's happening before your conscious brain catches up. This was one of those times. A piece of me knew it all along. Dorian had never been interested in visiting the catacombs with me. He hadn't been interested in the journal with an alchemical symbol. He'd only been interested in the illustration. He was far from stupid. He wasn't only obsessed with the illustration because it bore his likeness and might make it slightly more difficult for him to hide. His likeness was already famous.

I should have seen the signs of just how much Dorian had been manipulating me. He thought of himself as a modern-day Poirot, his detective of choice not because he spoke French but because Dorian, more than anyone, had "little gray cells." He loved coming up with complicated plans to solve mysteries. Ever since he'd read the entire Agatha Christie canon, he'd decided he was a better detective than Poirot. After all, he literally had "little gray cells." Yet he'd barely said a word about my illegal map of the catacombs.

"What do you mean," I began slowly, "you were never concerned about the backward alchemists?"

"The Victor Hugo illustration was always the key. Always. The professor knew the truth, until he was silenced. You did as well, until you were fooled."

"Fooled by what?"

"This fake illustration that appropriates the memory of the man who created me!"

Fake? Had he said fake?

"It was tested. Authenticated. You know this. Why did you still say it's fake?"

"Because there is fraud afoot. I believe this whole situation was a hoax!"

"A *hoax*?"

"A scam."

"I get it. I was repeating the word because I don't believe it."

"You must believe me that the exhibit was a fake! Claiming that bohemian author Victor Hugo was the person who envisioned me, *not* the revered architect Viollet-le-Duc? Impossible."

"It's true, you know."

Dorian sputtered but was unable to form words.

"It was Victor Hugo's novel that captured the imagination of the Parisian public," I said calmly, "and inspired the Gothic recreation of the cathedral, which included so many gargoyles that weren't there before. Without Victor Hugo, the cathedral wouldn't exist as it is today."

"Yes, yes, I know this," Dorian said, having recovered his voice. "Most people believe the cathedral's gargoyles and chimeras are medieval, yet they are very much mistaken. This is *not* what I am saying. I am asking: why, if this blasphemy were true, would his illustrations of gargoyles have been a secret until now?" He stomped his feet in frustration. "He was not a modest man."

Neither was Dorian. But he had a point.

"Lots of pieces of history get lost," I said, "as you and I both know better than most people. But if it's fake, it was planted more than a hundred years ago. That was an especially long con."

"It is not such a long time."

"*This* is why you wanted to come to France."

"I will," Dorian sniffed, "as you Americans say, *take the Fifth*."

I crossed my arms and glared at the gargoyle.

"How much do you know about Eugène Emmanuel Viollet-le-Duc?" Dorian asked.

"You think *Viollet-le-Duc* was involved in the fraud?"

"More blasphemy! No. Humor an old gargoyle. I am attempting to explain how I know this illustration is fake."

"Beyond what you've told me about Viollet-le-Duc giving his carving to your father, I read about him when he was awarded the commission for the Notre Dame renovation, along with his partner, um..."

"Jean-Baptiste Lassus. Yes. Lassus died before the renovation was complete, so his mark on the project was not as strong. Viollet-le-Duc was the man most closely involved in the creation of the new gallery of gargoyles. He drew three-dimensional illustrations of us with such life and personality. His sketches were used by the craftsmen who sculpted the figures of stone."

"Including you."

"I was more charming than the rest, you know," Dorian said with a straight face.

"Of course," I responded in kind.

"Yet I was too small to be seen from below, so Viollet-le-Duc gave me to his friend and started anew."

"I know all this, Dorian. Well, except for forgetting Lassus's name. Why are the architects important here?"

"I have never felt such emptiness and devastation as when we watched my birthplace burn. We were so far away and helpless. This is *who I am,* Zoe." His wings sagged, and his whole body curled inward. "I have a unique beginning, but at least I believed I knew what it was. Viollet-le-Duc envisioned me, and could not bear to destroy me even when I did not fit the vision for his restored cathedral. He knew his dear friend would appreciate me. They and the cathedral are my origin. And now someone wishes to cover that up. You can understand this, no?"

The man Dorian thought of as his father, Jean Eugène Robert-Houdin, is considered the father of modern stage magic. I was glad he wasn't as famous as Houdini, the escape artist born Eric Weiss who'd admired Robert-Houdin so much he'd taken the magician's name for his stage persona. If Robert-Houdin had been as famous as Houdini, I had no doubt an enterprising historian would have looked more carefully at his life and discovered that the secrecy he insisted upon in his later years wasn't to finish another memoir, but to raise a living gargoyle in secrecy.

No written records exist of the friendship between Notre Dame's famed restorer Viollet-le-Duc and Robert-Houdin, but Dorian's existence proves otherwise. Dorian's father told him the story of how Viollet-le-Duc had given the magician the carving because of his love of the dramatic and the macabre.

I did understand why Dorian cared so much, but that didn't justify him lying to me every step of the way on this muddled endeavor.

"You admit it's a fake?" he asked. "You will help me destroy it?"

"No. Oh!"

"I know this look on your face. What have you realized?"

"The fact that only the illustration was stolen makes me believe it's a fake."

"You speak in riddles, Alchemist."

"We've been equating the illustration and the journal this whole time. Everyone has been. But it was only the illustration that was stolen. I was flustered when I left Professor Boucher, so I didn't think carefully about what he'd told me. He said the journal is what had been scientifically authenticated. Not the illustration."

"They were supposedly found together," Dorian said, steepling his fingers together, "yet that does not mean they were created at the same time."

"No. And what better way to fake an illustration than to plant it inside a *real* historical journal?"

"It was art historians who authenticated the illustration," Dorian added, "not with science but with their interpretation, clouded by their desire for it to be real."

"Art historians like Marcel Boucher."

TWENTY-TWO

"The question," Dorian said, pacing the length of the small apartment, "is how we *prove* that the Lost Gargoyle of Paris is a fake. My original plan was simply to steal the fraudulent illustration myself, then hide in plain sight in stone form on the side of the building. Yet someone beat me to it."

"You would have destroyed it before being certain it was fake? Since we still don't know if our theory is correct."

He shrugged. "This was the moral thing to do. If it was fake, then such false information should not have been allowed to cloud the memory of Viollet-le-Duc. If it was a true illustration by Victor Hugo, it would have been too great a magnet for evil alchemists. Either way, the world is better off without it."

"I don't know how the thief stole it from the museum," I said, "but I have a way for us to figure out how someone planted their fake in the ruins of the cathedral in the first place."

"You do?"

"I didn't go as far as I could have gone in the catacombs, because I was by myself. I went as far as the backward alchemy lab, because that's what I thought I needed to know. But the tunnel went further."

#

"I suppose it is not so terrible to have been conceived by a celebrated author," Dorian said as we crept through the tunnels that night, "instead of an architectural genius. After all, Victor Hugo's book is the reason the cathedral before us exists today. Yet..."

"Yet?" I shone my flashlight from the damp wall to Dorian's gray face. The air was dank and the shadows harsh.

"Yet he is celebrated for writing *books*. Not *artwork*. Viollet-le-Duc's hand stretched beyond imagination and drew perfectly realized forms."

"It's entirely possible Victor Hugo made his sketch afterward," I said. "There wasn't anything referencing dates in the exhibit."

"Ah! This is a brilliant deduction. I am surprised you thought of it first. Yes. The novel touched the bosom of French citizens in the 1830s, inspiring all ranks of society, including my father and his architect friend. Did you know Viollet-le-Duc himself drew illustrations in an 1870s edition of *Notre-Dame de Paris*?"

I stooped and ducked under a low section of the tunnel. We were venturing deeper into a section of the catacombs where even the cataphiles feared to tread. There was no graffiti on these walls. No abandoned plastic water bottles on the ground.

"You forget you're not the only one in this room who was alive then," I said, wishing I'd brought some myrrh to make the rancid scent less unpleasant.

Dorian chuckled. "Yes, this is what must have happened. Victor Hugo made many drunken drawings, he would not have remembered the timing nor dated them. His true talent was pulling people into the romantic Paris of days gone by. A Paris when times were simpler. A time when common people could structure the rhythm of their lives around the sonorous sound of the bells of Notre Dame chiming. A time when —"

"A time that never existed," I cut in. "The 1480s weren't that great, you know."

"Even you, Alchemist, were not alive so many centuries ago. It was long before you were born. How do you know—"

"From what we know of history, you'd travel back to the Middle Ages if you could?"

He shuddered. Then gasped. "We have arrived?"

"Yes. You can feel it too?"

"*Oui.*"

"The backward alchemy lab." I whispered even though nobody could hear us.

"The lair of those lazy, lazy men."

"And women," I corrected.

A few steps beyond the secret abandoned underground alchemy lab, it was impossible to tell that such a room existed at all. If we hadn't known where it was, we never would have found it. Without my map, we couldn't have dared venture even further. As it was, after a few feet, the tunnel became so narrow we could barely fit.

I stopped and Dorian crashed into me.

"Are you too large to fit?" he asked, shaking out his wings. "I can continue without you. My physique is made for these rugged catacombs, *n'est-ce pas*?"

"That's not why I stopped. Look." I shone my flashlight on the ground.

"Footprints," Dorian whispered.

"Someone else has been here." I stepped forward, following the path of our phantom.

We walked in silence for only a few seconds before I stopped again. This time, Dorian was right. I could no longer fit into the small space.

We retreated until there was enough space for us to switch places. Dorian nodded gravely at me, tucked his wings securely behind his back, and stepped forward into the dark, narrow crevasse.

I kept my flashlight trained on the little gargoyle, holding my breath. How far would the tunnel stretch? And how could a person have fit in the narrow slice of tunnel? Had the footprints been those of a rebellious child playing games in the catacombs? What other possible explanation could there be?

"A dead end," Dorian called a few moments later, tapping his claws against the multicolored limestone deposits.

From my spot several yards away, I shone my flashlight along the dusty ground, now marred by Dorian's claw prints, to the back of his wings, and onward…

"No," I said. *As above, so below.* "It's not a dead end. Look up."

Nearly invisible in the stone ceiling above were four cracks. Only they weren't cracks. They were too even. This was a door.

"What are you doing?" I hissed.

"Seeing where the door leads. Do not worry, *mon amie.*" He grinned as he scooped up two hearty stones from the ground. "These will serve to keep the trap door open."

He scrambled up the wall and pushed. I didn't hear a sound, and could barely see what was happening, but I felt it. The air smelled thickly of smoke. A woody, earthy scent. Damp.

Dorian was inside the crypt of Notre Dame Cathedral.

Our phantom footprints had entered the cathedral from underground.

TWENTY-THREE

"What does it mean?" Dorian asked.

We were back at the apartment, and Dorian had fixed me a hot cocoa so I wouldn't fall asleep. I'm so sensitive to caffeine that anything with chocolate would keep me awake for hours.

"That an enterprising thief could have sneaked into the secured cathedral *after* the fire to plant something they wanted discovered."

Dorian shook his head and blew on his cocoa. "I have been putting my little gray cells to work since we crept back to the flat under cover of darkness, yet I cannot make sense of it. I do not believe so many people would be corrupt. Even with the moral argument that the auction would fetch so much money to rebuild the cathedral, there would be a broken link in the chain of deception. Someone would come forward."

"Only if they believed it was fraud. There would be no purposeful deception if they truly believed the journal and illustration had been unearthed because of the fire."

"Ah!"

"If someone stumbled upon the journal of a man who worked on the restoration of Notre Dame in the mid 1800s, perhaps in their attic, it might be worth several thousand dollars. Maybe tens of thousands, if the journal was something special. That's nothing compared to an illustration by Victor Hugo of a gargoyle of Notre Dame, at a time when the cathedral is in the spotlight. As you just said yourself, the illustration is what's being auctioned off, expected to raise millions."

"Yet it was stolen before the auction."

"*Before* it could be proven to be a fake. Which is why I'm more and more convinced you're right that the illustration is fake."

Dorian nodded. "I understand." Then he shook his head. "And yet at the same time, I do *not* understand."

"I don't know for certain that I'm right, because we don't know the whole story. But it's the only explanation that fits."

"The great detectives of the Golden Age of detective fiction have much to teach us. We must begin with the motive. This is what Agatha Christie teaches so sagely."

"A motive won't tell us how thieves disappeared from a locked museum. John Dickson Carr and Clayton Rawson would tell us this much."

Dorian dismissed the famous locked-room mystery writers with a twitch of his snout. "Dorothy Sayers would say we must look beyond motives and beyond mechanics—to human nature."

"That's all well and good in fiction, but for the real life problem at hand, it's a combination of all of those devices. It's…"

"*Mon amie?* Are you faint? Is it too late in the night? *Mon dieu*! My cocoa has had a soporific effect! How has this happened?"

"It's not that." I shook off the clawed fingers shaking my shoulders. "I think I know how he did it. And why."

"The art historian?"

"Yes. But not the one you think."

TWENTY-FOUR

"Carter?" Dorian repeated. He'd fixed me a second cup of cocoa, this one with extra cacao so I'd stay awake long enough to explain the truth I'd reasoned out.

"You were right about him," I said. "But not for the reason you thought."

"No twin?"

"No twin. But he didn't pull off the theft himself. He succeeded in accomplishing a seemingly impossible theft by convincing other people to help him. That's how he managed to have a dozen people as an alibi—including me!" I bristled as I remembered his fake-drunk act in the apartment building's beautiful courtyard garden.

Dorian narrowed his eyes. "Why would anyone help such a man?"

"He's a con man. I should have seen it sooner. Everything he did was perfectly planned. He left nothing to chance."

"Some things were chance," Dorian cut in. "This apartment building."

I shook my head. "It's not a coincidence that we and Carter are in the same building. This is the only apartment building with rental units with this particular view of the cathedral—which is why both you and Carter wanted rooms there. You wanted to be near the cathedral where you were born and we wanted to see whether the backward alchemists had returned. For Carter, my guess is so he could keep a lookout for any unexpected visitors as his accomplice slipped into the wreckage of Notre Dame from the catacombs to plant the fake journal and illustration."

"Ah, so..." Dorian murmured.

"I hate to say it, but Carter can be incredibly charming when he wants to be. I can easily believe he charmed women into helping him with his deception. There's one woman in particular I know I'm right about. She's the key to the supposedly impossible theft. You remember the woman I mentioned who was filming the police right after the theft, supposedly to see what they knew?"

"The late-night jogger."

"She was the thief."

"I did not see her enter—"

"Because she didn't. Not while you were watching. She had time to steal the illustration because she was never in a rush in the first place. She got inside the museum hours earlier by curling up in Carter's rolling bag. She hid in the cloakroom until the museum closed."

"Ah!" Dorian cried as comprehension dawned on him. "She set off the alarm when she *exited,* not when she entered. She would only need a few moments to blend in with the small crowd."

"I don't know exactly how Carter got through security with a petite woman inside his bag or how he forged the illustration. But he must have conned the security guard and an artist—unless he was that skilled an artist himself, which I doubt. Men like Carter have other people do the work for them."

"And," Dorian mused, "a successful con man would be able to sell the fake illustration on the black market to someone who would not have it authenticated. Because of how much everyone *wanted* to believe it was real, and because the proceeds would go to the restoration of Notre Dame Cathedral, he counted on the psychology of people not questioning too closely, after the journal itself was proved to be authentic. Yes, yes, this is all very good as a theoretical exercise. But how do you know for certain that the jogger was Carter's accomplice? There are many petite women in Paris."

"It's not only her diminutive size. Remember our burglar?"

"You said she was the cleaning woman who let herself into our apartment, and that I should not worry."

"I was wrong. That happened right at the moment when Carter said he needed just a few moments to grab his bag. You said she was small, wore sneakers, and inspected the bookshelf before leaving. You noticed the small box being used as a bookend had been moved—I think she took it."

"But why?"

"Carter has been careful every step of the way. It makes sense he would have left anything incriminating in the attic directly above his apartment, in case things went wrong and his own rental was searched. I expected that box was a real antique and meant to house the illustration for the illicit buyer. Remember how surprised he was that there was another guest staying in this section of the apartment building. The attic wasn't supposed to be rented out. That's why it was so dusty, and why it hadn't been on the market for rent until you convinced the manager to rent the apartment to me. That happened after Carter had inquired to make sure he was the only one at the top floor of the building and that nobody was in the attic apartment."

Dorian steepled his fingers together and nodded silently. "Your theories are sound. I am convinced. And ashamed that I did not make these connections! Though to be fair, you are the one who spent time with the culprit. Yes, the more I think of it, there was no way for me to make these deductions."

I suppressed a smile. Dorian's ego was intact.

"Yet," Dorian continued, "your brilliant deductions will not be enough for the authorities. Professor Boucher has accused you of involvement in the theft to *les flics*. We need proof."

"Then it's a good thing I have a plan."

The next morning, I staked out the apartment beginning at dawn to put it into place.

At least, I'd do so if Carter ever woke up and left the apartment. That was the problem with con men. They were creatures of the night. I only hoped I wasn't a day late to catch this one.

TWENTY-FIVE

I was on my second cup of holy basil tea and had long since finished one of Dorian's homemade scones when Carter stepped into the courtyard.

"Good morning, Carter."

"Zoe." He blushed. "I'm so sorry I blundered your name so royally while I was drunk the night before last."

"I don't think you were really that drunk."

He clutched his hand to his heart. "Again, you wound me. You think I could be such a buffoon while sober?"

"Make it up to me," I said.

He grinned. "How?"

"Buy me breakfast."

"Now?"

"You're not busy, are you?"

He glanced at his phone. "For a beautiful woman, I can always make time."

"I knew you could."

"How about the cafe across the street?"

"I thought you'd suggest that one."

We crossed the street to the cafe with a red and white striped awning and small tables that ensured only the daintiest of meals could be enjoyed on them.

"I'm impressed," I said.

He laughed. "I know. My ability to order a croissant and an espresso in French is pretty impressive."

"Not about that. About the impossible crime. The whole thing, really."

"I don't know what you're—"

"The complexity of the whole thing. You had to plan it perfectly, and you did it more brilliantly than anyone I've ever seen. I wasn't kidding about being impressed."

"I still don't have the faintest idea what you're talking about," he said. But this time, the tone of his voice had changed. And his expression. The surprise in his eyes transformed into curiosity.

"That's a shame," I said.

"Who *are you*, Zoe Faust?"

"I find the question of who is Carter Dickson to be far more interesting, don't you? Nice pseudonym, by the way."

I was rewarded with half a smile. "My surname was on the museum ticket."

"That ticket that also explains the method for your crime."

"Me? I've committed no crimes." He was grinning as he shook his head. "Still, we wouldn't want anyone getting the wrong idea, would we? May I see your phone?"

I handed it to him. He shut it off and removed the sim card.

"I hate to ask," he added, "but phones aren't the only things capable of recording."

I stood up, slipped out of my silver coat, and held my arms out. He was a gentleman as he patted me down. Onlookers didn't give us a second glance. Public displays of affection were so common here that nobody thought anything of it. Our waiter didn't even bat an eye as he delivered Carter's espresso and croissant, and my tea and *chausson aux pommes.*

"I'm surprised you don't have someone else to confide in," I said.

"That wouldn't do, would it?"

I gave out an involuntary gasp.

"What?" he said. "My accent? It took quite some time to perfect that American one. I'm glad it was so successful."

I couldn't place his new accent. Not exactly. It was a blend of multiple countries.

"I'll satisfy your curiosity if you satisfy mine," he added. "How did you end up staying one floor above me? I know you're not police."

"You wouldn't believe me if I told you."

"Try me."

I shrugged. "I'm friends with one of the gargoyles of Notre Dame. He suggested the apartment, since it's the only building of affordable vacation rentals with such a perfect, unobstructed view of the cathedral."

He sipped his espresso as he studied my face. "You win. I'm not going to get the truth out of you. I know when I've met my match. At least answer me truthfully about one thing. The boyfriend. Is he real?"

"Very much so."

"My loss."

"Don't you already have your hands full? I'm guessing you were dating all three of them. Am I right?"

His face froze, but only for a moment. "Only little Lucy. And it's a casual thing. She's a wild one. But the others? God, no."

"How did you convince Paloma Orleans to forge the illustration, then?" I took a bite of the sweet apple pastry.

"It's my turn to be impressed, Zoe. Where did I go wrong?"

"You didn't. Not with Madame Orleans, the descendant of the stonemason. Her donating the journal and illustration gave me the answer to *why* you did it—to sell a forged illustration that wouldn't be questioned since her family's journal was indeed real—but it was the woman you called Little Lucy that told me *how*. It was very clever of you to have her curl up inside your suitcase, and to have the guard at the museum be in on it."

"The guard was the weakest link. Blackmail is never pretty."

"The others were easy?"

He smiled. "For someone like me. I convinced Paloma Orleans that her generosity in donating her great grandfather's journal would help launch her into artistic stardom. She'd always felt she'd been overlooked as an artist, like her ancestor who was a stone worker at Notre Dame."

"And Lucy?"

"I convinced her I was in love with her. Don't look at me like that. It's mostly true. She's very acrobatic."

I tried not to roll my eyes. I glanced at my useless phone, sitting on the table next to my tea.

"Am I boring you?" he asked.

"Hardly. I was hoping for confirmation of something, but without my phone, that's not possible. It doesn't matter. I think it's been long enough that I don't need to worry."

"What do you mean?" He glanced at the entry to our apartment complex, in clear view. No authorities, or anyone besides the chatty Australian I'd met the other night, had entered or exited while we'd been at the cafe.

I followed his gaze. "I'm sorry you won't be able to see the fruition of your well-laid plan."

His face grew pale. He leapt up from the table, leaving me to pay the bill. I didn't mind. The plainclothes police officer seated two tables over, who I'd convinced to be at the café that morning, gave chase.

#

The police officer caught up with Carter Dickson next to the fountain in the courtyard. I waved as I walked past as Carter was hauled away in handcuffs. I'd agreed to make a full statement later that day. It was a relief Carter had confessed in front of the officer. If not, professor Boucher's own statements against me would have made things awfully tricky.

After two breakfasts, I opted for the stairs instead of the elevator.

I found Dorian in our rental unit, where he'd been stress-baking all morning until Carter left his apartment. Then, while I'd kept Carter busy across the street, Dorian had stolen the fake illustration by sneaking down the drainpipe and in through the window.

"Your plan succeeded?" he asked.

"He was arrested downstairs."

Dorian smiled and popped a truffle into his mouth. "And the illustration? It is a forgery?"

"It is."

"I may destroy it, then?"

"Let's take things one step at a time. The police might need it."

"As long as it does not take too long." Dorian scampered to the window and peeked out at the cathedral. "I will always love Paris, but I am ready to go home."

THE END

Turn the page for vegan recipes and an Author's Note that explains fact versus fiction (hint—most of the history in *The Lost Gargoyle of Paris* is true).

Sign up for Gigi's email newsletter at www.gigipandian.com to stay up to date—plus receive a free novella when you sign up.

RECIPES

Chia seed pancakes (vegan)

I was going to include a recipe for the crêpes Dorian made, but then thought better of it. I want all of the recipes I include in my books to be as user-friendly as possible, and crêpes are difficult to get right. Instead, here's a recipe for a cousin of the crêpe: pancakes. This is my current favorite pancake recipe.

Total cooking time: 20 minutes
Makes 2 servings: 4 large pancakes or 8 small ones

Ingredients

- 1/2 cup whole wheat flour
- 1 Tbsp chia seeds
- 1 tsp baking powder
- dash salt
- 3/4 cup oat milk or nut milk of choice
- 1 heaping Tbsp almond butter
- 1 Tbsp maple syrup

Directions

Mix the dry ingredients together in a small bowl, then whisk the wet ingredients into the mixture (including the maple syrup). Let the batter rest for 10 minutes to allow the chia seeds to plump. Heat a small amount of oil in a skillet on medium heat. Once the pan is hot, use a small ladle to form pancakes. Cook for approx. 2 - 3 minutes per side, until golden brown.

Variation: Stir 1/4 cup fresh blueberries or berry of choice into the batter immediately before cooking.

Béchamel Sauce (vegan)

Béchamel sauce is a creamy sauce, known as one of the French "mother sauces," which can easily be made dairy-free. It's a versatile sauce that can be used in lasagna, moussaka, potato gratin, or as an easy pasta sauce or creamy soup base—or, as Dorian did in this novella, simply drizzled over roasted vegetables.

Total cooking time: 20 minutes
Serving size will vary depending on how you use it

Ingredients

- 3 Tbsp olive oil
- 3 Tbsp white flour, sifted
- 2-1/2 cups oat milk or nut milk of choice (note: rice milk does not work well here)
- 1/4 tsp salt
- 1/4 tsp freshy grated nutmeg

Directions

Heat the oil in a saucepan. Over medium heat, slowly add the sifted flour, and whisk quickly. This creates a roux - a thickening mixture that's equal parts butter or oil and flour. Once fully mixed, whisk in a few tablespoons of the milk. Once that small amount of liquid binds with the roux, add the rest more quickly. Continue to stir over medium heat until the sauce thickens. It should take about 15 minutes. Add the salt and freshy grated nutmeg.

It's now ready to use as a quick topping for pasta or vegetables, by adding just a pinch more salt and pepper, or as a base for a more complex dish.

Variation: Add a deeper savory flavor by sautéing half of an onion and two cloves of garlic in the olive oil before whisking in the flour.

Author's Note

Most of the history described in *The Lost Gargoyle of Paris* is true. Notre Dame Cathedral does contain many hidden alchemical symbols carved in its stone façade, though there isn't a secret alchemy lab in the catacombs beneath the city (as far as we know).

French architect-restorers Eugène Viollet-Le-Duc and his partner Jean Baptiste Lassus created their mid-nineteenth-century restoration of Notre Dame only after Victor Hugo's *Notre-Dame de Paris* had imagined a romantic Gothic building filled with gargoyles that had never existed in reality. When Violet-le-Duc illustrated a later volume of Hugo's novel, he included his gargoyles that hadn't existed in the Middle Ages. Hugo was also a gifted artist, but it was a talent he kept hidden for much of his life.

Other real historical figures mentioned are Nicolas Flamel, Perenelle Flamel, and Jean Eugène Robert-Houdin. However, there's no evidence that Robert-Houdin was a friend of Viollet-le-Duc, nor is there proof that Nicolas and Perenelle Flamel were true alchemists (although their graves were found to be empty when exhumed…).

For further reading, I highly recommend the nonfiction book *The Gargoyles of Notre Dame* by Michael Camille. That book is the reason why *The Lost Gargoyle of Paris* ended up being a novella instead of the short story I initially imagined. When the tragic fire swept through Notre Dame Cathedral on April 15, 2019, many of my readers wrote to me saying they thought of Zoe and the backward alchemists from *The Elusive Elixir* (book 3 in the series), and I knew I had to send her back.

For those of you who are new to the series, I'll answer the question I get asked all the time: Why a vegan gargoyle chef?

I began writing the series when I was 36 years old and undergoing chemotherapy for an aggressive breast cancer. At the time, I didn't consider myself a cook. But during my recovery, I learned what a big difference healing foods made in my life. Through cooking classes, cookbooks, and kitchen experimentation, I learned that plant-based cooking can taste more amazing than anything I used to eat, and I felt healthier than ever before. During chemo, I was writing for myself, not for an audience, so as a life-long classic mystery fan who was fascinated by mysterious gargoyles, I created a fun gargoyle character. I doubted anyone besides me would get a kick out of Dorian. I was happily proven wrong.

I'm now eight years cancer free. There are four full-length novels out in the Accidental Alchemist series so far, with many more to follow.

About the Author

Gigi Pandian is a *USA Today* bestselling and award-winning mystery author, breast cancer survivor, and accidental almost-vegan. The child of cultural anthropologists from New Mexico and the southern tip of India, she spent her childhood traveling around the world on research trips and now lives outside San Francisco with her husband and a gargoyle who watches over the garden. Gigi writes the Jaya Jones Treasure Hunt mysteries, the Accidental Alchemist mysteries, and locked-room mystery short stories. Her debut novel, *Artifact*, was awarded a Malice Domestic Grant, and her mysteries have received Agatha, Rose, Lefty, and Derringer awards.

Made in the USA
Middletown, DE
04 July 2021